MANDIE®
AND THE
UNWANTED
GIFT

Mandie® Mysteries

MANDIE®
AND THE
UNWANTED
GIFT

Lois Gladys Leppard

BETHANY HOUSE PUBLISHERS
MINNEAPOLIS, MINNESOTA 55438

Mandie and the Unwanted Gift
Copyright © 1997
Lois Gladys Leppard

MANDIE® is a registered trademark of
Lois Gladys Leppard

Library of Congress Catalog Card Number
97–33827

ISBN 1–55661–556–6

Cover illustration by Chris Wold Dyrud

Published by Bethany House Publishers
11400 Hampshire Avenue South
Bloomington, Minnesota 55438
www.bethanyhouse.com

Bethany House Publishers is a Division of
Baker Book House Company, Grand Rapids, Michigan.

Printed in the United States of America

Especially for—
Dr. and Mrs. Jack (Phinalia) Hunter,
owners of Lemstone Books, Spartanburg, S.C.
With love and thanks
for all their support throughout the years

About the Author

LOIS GLADYS LEPPARD worked in Federal Intelligence for thirteen years in various countries around the world. She now makes her home in South Carolina.

The stories of her mother's childhood as an orphan in western North Carolina are the basis for many of the incidents incoporated in this series.

Visit her Web site: www.Mandie.com

Contents

"No idleness, no laziness, no procrastination;
never put off till tomorrow
what you can do today."

—from Lord Chesterfield's "Letters"
December 26, 1749

Chapter 1 / Home!

"Here comes Ben," Mandie told Celia Hamilton as they stood in the window of the Misses Heathwood's School for Girls in Asheville, North Carolina. She reached back to the chair behind her, picked up her winter coat, and hurriedly put it on.

"Are you going to tell your grandmother?" Celia asked as Mandie placed her blue tam on her blond head and pulled on her matching gloves.

Mandie sighed loudly as she looked at her friend. "I suppose I'll have to sooner or later, but I dread doing it," she replied.

"Yes, you do have to, Mandie, and the sooner you tell her the better," Celia said. "Oh, how I wish I could go home with you for Christmas. I'd sure like to know what the repercussions are. You're going to have some interesting holidays."

"Maybe you could ask your mother just one more time. Maybe she would finally agree to come to our house. You never know," Mandie replied as she picked up her small purse from the chair.

"Mother might agree for her and me to come, but Aunt Rebecca won't," Celia said. "She says she has so many things to do for the holidays, and Mother won't go off and leave her because she does live with us, you know."

"I have to go now. I hear Ben in the hallway, and I need to show him my baggage," Mandie said as she reached to squeeze her friend's hand. "I hope you have a wonderful Christmas, Celia. I'll see you when we come back to school the day after New Year's. I hope your Aunt Rebecca's train gets in on time so you can get on home."

Celia squeezed Mandie's hand and said, "You mean so we can catch the next train going back. You see how nice Aunt Rebecca is to me. She comes all the way here from Richmond just to travel back home with me so my mother won't have to make the trip."

"I know. I wish I had an aunt like that, but I don't have an aunt at all," Mandie said. She released Celia's hand to go out into the hallway to look for her grandmother's driver, Ben. Glancing back at her friend, she said, "Good-bye, and Merry Christmas and Happy New Year. I'll see you in 1902."

"Same to you, Mandie," Celia called after her. "Don't forget to tell your grandmother. Also, you should prepare Joe for the forthcoming event."

Mandie sighed and looked around the hallway where the other schoolgirls were standing about, waiting to be picked up for their journeys home for the holidays. She spotted Aunt Phoebe, the school's housekeeper, pointing to Mandie's trunk as Ben went toward it.

"Here I am, Ben," Mandie called to the man,

who smiled at her as he bent over to pick up the trunk. Hurrying over to the old woman, Mandie quickly hugged her and said, "Merry Christmas, Aunt Phoebe. I've already seen everyone else, and I was afraid I was going to miss you."

"Merry Christmas to you," Aunt Phoebe replied as she returned the hug. "You hurry back, now. Gonna be awfully quiet round here wid all you girls gone."

"Then you'll be able to get some rest. Bye now," Mandie told her, smiling and hurrying after Ben, who was going out the front door.

She followed Ben to her grandmother's carriage that was parked in the long driveway. As she got in, Ben put the trunk on the back and called to her, "Miz Taft, she say hurry now so y'all don't miss dat train." He jumped up on the seat.

Mandie knew Ben liked to drive fast when her grandmother wasn't around. He raced the carriage through the cobblestone streets of Asheville and pulled up at her grandmother's huge mansion before she could sort out her thoughts. She knew she would have to tell her grandmother about what she had done, and Celia was right, the sooner the better. She quickly stepped down from the vehicle and hurried to the house.

Ella, the maid, opened the heavy carved wooden door with stained-glass panels as Mandie stepped up onto the front porch. "Miz Taft, she say hurry," she told Mandie. "Gotta eat a bite 'fo you goes to de depot."

"Thank you, Ella," Mandie said. She removed her coat and hat and hung them on the hall tree. "Where is Grandmother?" She looked around the hallway. "And where is Snowball?"

"Yo' grandma, she be in de dinin' room waitin' fo' you, and dat white cat, he be eatin' in de kitchen," Ella explained. "Now, git on wid you. Hurry."

Mandie smiled at the girl and hurried to the dining room. Mrs. Taft was putting food on her plate from the sideboard. "Get a plate, Amanda," she said as she glanced at Mandie. "And please hurry."

Mandie quickly picked up a plate, spooned bites of food on it, and followed her grandmother to the table where they sat down.

"Is the train going to be early, Grandmother? Is that why we have to rush so? It's not supposed to be here for another two hours," Mandie said, dipping into the food with her fork.

"No, dear, it's supposed to be on the regular schedule," Mrs. Taft explained as she hurriedly ate. "It's just that I have to pick up some packages down at Wharton's Store, and Ben will have to open my trunk and put them inside before we can get on the train."

Mandie looked at her grandmother and said, "Packages? Hmm! Like Christmas presents?" She smiled.

Mrs. Taft smiled back and said, "Yes, like Christmas presents, and don't ask me anything else. We won't discuss it."

"I will have to buy some things to give certain people when I get home," Mandie said with a mysterious smile.

"Oh dear, there's not much of a selection in Franklin. You should have done your Christmas shopping here in Asheville," Mrs. Taft told her.

"But I would have had too many presents to pack and take home," Mandie reminded her. "After all, there's Mother, Uncle John, Aunt Lou, Liza, Jenny, Abraham, Mr. Bond, Uncle Ned, and—"

"Never mind, dear," Mrs. Taft interrupted her. "I'm aware that there are quite a few people you give to, but just eat up now so we can be on our way."

Mandie knew this was not the time to talk to her grandmother, so she put it off. Maybe on the train she would have the right opportunity to tell her what she had done. She had written to her mother and told her, and Elizabeth had replied that it was all right. She hoped her mother would help her out when she told Mrs. Taft. She was worried that her grandmother would become angry and pack up and go back home.

And then she thought about her friend Joe Woodard. Joe was jealous of her. In fact, he had asked her to marry him when they grew up, and now at the age of thirteen Mandie smiled as she remembered the occasion. It happened during the day her mother, Elizabeth, had married John Shaw, brother to Mandie's father, Jim Shaw, who had died last year. Sharp pains shot through Mandie's heart as she remembered losing her father, but she had been happy when her mother married John. Joe had become possessive of Mandie beginning that day. And now Mandie knew there was bound to be some friction during the holidays when Joe and his parents came for their usual Christmas visit.

"Amanda," Mrs. Taft spoke sharply, bringing Mandie back to the present. "Are you going to finish that food?"

"Oh, I'm sorry, Grandmother," Mandie quickly replied as she began cramming the food into her mouth. "I was thinking about something."

"Well, right now we'd better think about getting to the store and on to the depot," Mrs. Taft reminded her.

They made it to Wharton's Store, picked up the packages, and Ben put them in Mrs. Taft's trunk. Then they got to the depot on time. Later, when they were on the train going to Franklin where Mandie lived with her mother and her uncle John, Mrs. Taft removed her hat and put a pillow behind her head. "I'd like to rest for a while, Amanda. Please don't let that cat get loose," she said.

"I won't, Grandmother," Mandie replied, glancing down at Snowball curled up on her bag at her feet. "I have his leash on, and I'll be sure to keep a tight rein on that."

If her grandmother was going to rest, Mandie wouldn't be able to talk to her and explain what she had done. Somewhat relieved at not having to discuss the matter, Mandie wrapped the end of Snowball's leash around her wrist and got comfortable herself. Soon she dozed off and slept the rest of the trip.

"Franklin! Franklin! All out for Franklin!" the conductor called as he walked through the car.

Mandie quickly sat up, rubbed her eyes, and found Snowball had jumped up into her lap. He stretched and began meowing. "Snowball, we're home," Mandie said as she set the white cat on the floor and held on to his leash.

"My, my, I must have been asleep," Mrs. Taft said. She sat up straight, put on her hat, and stood up as the train came to a halt.

Mandie rose, looked through the window, and said, "I see Mr. Jason out there. I thought maybe Uncle John would come to pick us up."

"Your uncle John is a busy man with all his business matters to look after. Let's go now," Mrs. Taft told Mandie. She picked up the small bag she had brought on the train and led the way to the door.

Mandie looped the handle of her bag on her arm, held on to Snowball, and followed.

"It's nice to see you, Mr. Bond," Mrs. Taft told the tall, gray-haired man as he assisted her down the train steps.

"Thank you, ma'am. It's always a pleasure to have you visit, I'm sure," Jason Bond told her. Turning to Mandie, he said, "Your uncle John had to go to Sylva on business, so he sent me to pick y'all up."

"Mr. Jason, do we have any company yet?" Mandie asked as she and Mrs. Taft followed him to John Shaw's carriage and got inside.

"Why, no, nobody," Jason Bond told her. "I suppose you are expecting a lot of people for Christmas, but nobody has arrived yet."

Mandie blew out a breath of relief and relaxed for the short ride to her home after Mr. Bond loaded their trunks on the back of the vehicle.

Mandie's mother, Elizabeth, met them at the front door. She quickly hugged her mother and then Mandie. Looking around she asked, "Did you not bring Hilda with you?" Hilda was the girl Mrs. Taft had taken into her home after Hilda's parents had given up on ever keeping her from running away. They claimed Hilda was not able to talk, although she was almost as old as Mandie.

Mrs. Taft and Mandie quickly removed their coats and hats and hung them on the hall tree. Snowball scampered away down the hall.

"No, Elizabeth," Mrs. Taft replied. "The Mannings wanted her to stay with them for Christmas to be company for their daughter. She broke her ankle, so they can't go anywhere for the holidays."

"I'm so sorry," Elizabeth replied and then said to Mandie, "I missed you at Thanksgiving, dear."

"And I missed you, Mother, but that was the only way I could go to New York, you know, just go straight back to school from New York," Mandie said, smiling up at the woman who was an older likeness of herself. "I've just got to tell you and Uncle John about the trip. I couldn't tell everything in the letter I wrote y'all."

"Well, right now let's go sit by the fire and get warm," Mrs. Taft said. "I do declare, Elizabeth, you are just going to have to get one of those furnaces installed, like they're putting in Amanda's school. The house would be so much more comfortable."

As the three of them walked toward the parlor, Elizabeth asked, "Have you had one put in your house, Mother?"

"Not yet, but I'm planning to," Mrs. Taft replied. She led the way into the parlor and went directly to a chair by the huge open fireplace, with logs blazing away inside.

"Oh, Mother, they make holes all over the place—in the walls and in the floors, and the rats can come in," Mandie said. She sat on a stool by her mother, who had taken the chair opposite Mrs. Taft.

"Yes, I understand why they have to do that," Elizabeth said. Then she turned to her mother and said, "John and I have been talking about getting a furnace. It would make the house warmer, but I understand from the Campbells that these things take a lot of work just to keep the fire in them going."

"There are different kinds of furnaces, Elizabeth," Mrs. Taft said. "If you pay enough to get a good one, there's some contraption to it that allows the coal to go into the firebox as it's needed."

"Well, I do hope you don't get the kind like they have in Edwards' Drygoods Store in Asheville. The radiators hiss and pop and make a terrible noise sometimes," Mandie said. "If they put a noisy radiator like that in our room at school, I don't know how Celia and I will ever sleep at night."

"Speaking of Celia, I wrote to her mother and asked if they would come visit for the Christmas holidays, and she said they couldn't leave Rebecca alone for Christmas," Elizabeth said to Mandie. "But I suppose we're going to have a houseful of people anyway, with the Woodards all coming and—"

"I know," Mandie quickly interrupted her mother. Then she hurried to say, "Mother, I will have to do some shopping for presents."

"I haven't finished buying everything I need, either, dear," Elizabeth said. "Maybe we can go downtown together tomorrow." Looking at Mrs. Taft, she added, "And you, too, of course, Mother."

"No, thank you," Mrs. Taft said. "I have mine all bought, wrapped, and waiting in my trunk. I'm not anxious to get in the crowds of shoppers."

Mandie did some quick thinking. She still couldn't get up the nerve to tell her grandmother what she had done, and she certainly didn't want her mother to give it away, but on the other hand, she couldn't stick with the two women every minute. She must watch for an opportunity to let her mother know she had not told her grandmother. So she would just have to separate them somehow.

Her thoughts were interrupted by Liza, the young maid, appearing at the door just then with a loaded tea cart that she pushed into the parlor.

"Oh, Liza, I'm so glad to see you," Mandie said, jumping up to rush and squeeze Liza's hand.

Liza smiled at her and said, "And I sho' am glad to be seein' you, Missy 'Manda. House been too quiet whilst you been gone."

Mandie laughed and said, "I'll be here until the day after New Year's, and then I have to go back to school. I've got to tell you all about New York. Liza, it's huge! And crammed full of people everywhere."

"You don't say!" Liza exclaimed and then added, "But I got to go back to de kitchen right now 'fo Aunt Lou come lookin' fo' me." Turning to Mandie's mother, she asked, "Miz 'Lizbeth, do everything look all right on dis heah cart?"

"Everything looks fine, Liza," Elizabeth replied, standing up to pour coffee from the pot. "You go on back to the kitchen and I'll take care of this."

"Yessum," Liza said as she started out the door.

"And, Liza, would you please tell Aunt Lou and all the others I'll see them in a little while?" Mandie asked.

"I sho' will, and I'll tell dem you gwine tell us all 'bout dat big place called Noo Yawk," Liza said as she smiled and went on out the door.

As soon as everyone had a cup of coffee and a sweet cake, John Shaw came into the parlor.

"Well, well, looks like I'm in time to join in," he said, going directly to the coffeepot and pouring himself a cup. Looking at Mrs. Taft, he said, "Glad you could come. We always look forward to seeing you."

"Thank you, John. It's always a pleasure to visit

with y'all," Mrs. Taft replied.

"And how's my little blue eyes?" he asked Mandie as he sat down nearby with the cup of coffee.

"Just fine, Uncle John. I'm always ready for holidays and a chance to come home," Mandie told him. "Especially Christmastime."

"With all the guests that go with it, no doubt," John Shaw said with a smile. "And I do believe we have quite a few coming to stay this year. The Woodards, Uncle Ned, and—"

"I know," Mandie interrupted him and then, smiling, added, "Just think. I don't have to be back to school until next year, 1902."

"But the second day of the year, if I remember correctly," Uncle John said with a nod.

"You got back home sooner than you expected, John. Were you able to take care of everything?" Elizabeth asked.

"Oh yes, all accomplished," John told her with a big wink.

Mandie, forever listening and looking for a mystery, frowned as she heard their conversation. What were her mother and Uncle John up to? Evidently they had some secret going between them. She glanced at her grandmother, but Mrs. Taft was absorbed in eating her sweet cake and was not in on the conversation. *Oh well*, she thought, *I can always find out lots of things just by remaining silent most of the time.*

"I thought we'd go find a nice Christmas tree after Joe gets here tomorrow," Uncle John told her.

"So the Woodards are coming tomorrow. That'll be fine, Uncle John," Mandie replied.

"Yes, Dr. Woodard has a patient or two he wants to drop in on in this area, so they're coming to visit tomorrow and will be here until New Year's if things don't get busy for him in other parts of the country," John Shaw said. "Now, the other guests—"

Mandie quickly stood up and set her cup and plate on the table nearby. "I think I'll go to the kitchen and see everyone, and then go upstairs and change clothes," she said, glancing at her grandmother, who seemed to be comfortable in the big chair. She started out the door.

"All right, dear. We're planning on supper at six tonight," Elizabeth said. "Polly Cornwallis and her mother will be over to join us, so please don't forget."

"Polly and her mother are coming to eat with us tonight?" Mandie questioned as she looked back into the room from the doorway. "Polly left school yesterday, a day early, so she and her mother could visit some relatives somewhere or other. They must have come on home."

"I believe they had a change in plans. But, anyhow, I spoke to Polly's mother this morning and invited them over tonight," Elizabeth explained.

"Oh well," Mandie said with a sigh. "I'll remember." She wasn't particularly fond of her next-door neighbor, Polly Cornwallis.

Mandie hurried down the long corridor to the kitchen. She could smell delicious odors coming from behind the closed door. And suddenly she felt starved.

She pushed open the door and was greeted by Aunt Lou, Jenny the cook, and Liza, who were all working around the big iron cookstove. Jenny's husband, Abraham, was stoking the firebox on the stove. Snowball was asleep in the wood box.

"There's my chile," Aunt Lou said, coming to embrace Mandie.

"I'm so glad to be home," Mandie said, returning the hug and then going to squeeze Jenny's free hand. "And to see everybody—Aunt Lou, Jenny, and Abraham, you, too. I've already seen Liza." She stepped over near the old man and added, "And guess what, Abraham? I saw your friend Dr. Plumbley in New York."

Abraham straightened up, looked at her, and said, "Is dat so? How he be, Missy? He comin' down dis way when it git warm weather?"

"He said he was," Mandie told him, and turning back to look at all the others, she became excited as she began relating her adventures in New York with Celia Hamilton and her mother during the Thanksgiving holiday. "You just can't imagine how big the place is and how many people are living inside that one town."

All the servants were listening to every word.

"And the Guyers have this enormous mansion so big we kept getting lost in it! And that hotel we stayed in at first had one thousand rooms in it," she explained, wide-eyed with her story. "Can you imagine that? One thousand rooms in one building?"

"Lawsy mercy, Missy, I couldn't count dat many rooms," Jenny said as she held a spoon over the boiling pot on the stove.

"How many people dey got cleanin' up all dat big building?" Liza asked, holding the lid to another pot in her hand.

Aunt Lou had opened the oven to check on a roast inside, and she straightened up to ask, "Why do my chile want to go to dat Yankee place?"

Mandie laughed and said, "Because I wanted to see what the place looked like and how the people up there live. Some of it is filled with huge mansions, but a good part of the town is full of poor people and terrible slums, pitiful people. Some of them can't even speak English."

Aunt Lou closed the oven door and turned to Mandie. "And when do dem Yankee friends of my chile plan to arrive heah?" she asked.

"Oh, so you know that Mr. Guyer and Jonathan are coming to visit us for the Christmas holidays!" Mandie exclaimed. "Please don't tell grandmother. She doesn't know yet."

"Why you not want huh to know?" Liza asked. "She gwine see dem when dey gits heah."

"I know, Liza, but I have to tell her first," Mandie quickly replied. "I sorta think my grandmother doesn't like Jonathan's father for some reason, and therefore she may not like the idea of them spending the holidays here with us. So I have to talk to her and try to persuade her to at least be nice to them."

"Dat's easier said den done, my chile," Aunt Lou said as she shook her head in dismay.

"Yo' gramma done sot in huh ways. I be thinkin' dis is gwine be a feisty Christmas," Jenny said as she turned to stir the contents of the pot.

"And I have another problem," Mandie said with a big sigh.

The servants paused to look at her.

"Seems you ain't got nuthin' but problems today," Abraham muttered.

"You all know Joe Woodard and his parents will be here during the whole week, beginning tomorrow according to Uncle John," Mandie said. "Well, you see, Joe Woodard and Jonathan Guyer don't like each other, either."

Everyone gasped, and Liza grinned and said, "And you gotta problem, too, Missy 'Manda. Dat Miss Sweet Thing next do', she gwine be home all Christmastime, and she gwine be settin' dem black eyes on de doctuh's son. Jes' you waits and see."

Mandie felt her face flush as she thought about the way Polly always seemed to trail after her and Joe. "Oh, Liza, I'm not worried about that," she replied. "And I'll have to figure out some way when Joe arrives tomorrow to let him know that Jonathan is also coming. And I still have to talk to my grandmother about the Guyers."

"Bettuh git busy and do dat' 'fo dem people gits heah," Aunt Lou warned her.

"I've got to go upstairs and change clothes. Maybe Grandmother has gone to her room and I can talk to her about it," Mandie said as she turned to leave the room.

"Let us know if we kin he'p in all dis mess you got yo'self into, my chile," Aunt Lou called after her.

"Thanks. I don't know what y'all can do, but I'll let you know," Mandie said as she hurried into the hallway.

She had to talk to her grandmother before the Guyers arrived, and she had not been able to ask her mother or Uncle John when they would get there. This was going to be an exciting, and maybe a miserable, Christmas.

Chapter 2 / More Questions

Mandie hurried down the upstairs hallway to the room her grandmother always occupied when she came to visit. The door was closed. She was probably inside.

"Grandmother," Mandie called as she gently tapped on the closed door. "Grandmother, could I speak to you for just a minute?"

There was the sound of movement inside the room, and then Mrs. Taft replied without opening the door, "Amanda, please see me later, dear. I'm getting changed for supper."

"Oh shucks!" Mandie said aloud to herself, and then answered, "All right, Grandmother. I'll see you later. I have to get dressed, too."

"Fine," Mrs. Taft called back.

Mandie hurried to her own room. She stepped inside and closed the door. Then she thought about finding her mother and asking exactly when the Guyers were arriving. Glancing at the china clock on the mantelpiece, she saw it was already twenty minutes past five. She didn't have time. It would have to wait.

Quickly flipping through her clothes hanging in the tall wardrobe, she took down a blue plaid wool dress. Even though there was a fire blazing away in the fireplace in the room, she felt cold as she thought about the problem of the Guyers coming for the holidays.

As Mandie started to change her clothes, a loud meow and a scratch at the bottom of the door told her Snowball was outside. She quickly let him into the room. He jumped up on the tall bed and walked in circles before he finally settled down in the middle and curled up.

"Snowball, I believe you're glad to be home, too," Mandie said, reaching to rub his white head.

The cat looked up at her and purred.

"And Christmas is next Wednesday, which means you'll have all kinds of good things to eat," Mandie added, continuing to pat his head. Snowball wasn't interested in anything but going to sleep. He moved his head away from her hand, curled up tighter, and closed his eyes.

As soon as Mandie was dressed, she rushed back down to the parlor, hoping to catch her mother or Uncle John to find out when the Guyers would be arriving. The room was empty. She kept walking back and forth from the warmth of the fireplace to the door to watch the hallway. Maybe her mother or Uncle John would get back before her grandmother did. On her dozenth trip to the doorway, she finally saw them coming down the hallway, but Mrs. Taft was with them.

"Oh shucks!" Mandie muttered to herself.

"You certainly dressed in a hurry, Amanda," Mrs. Taft said as she entered the room and went to sit by the fireplace.

"And you certainly do look pretty, dear," Elizabeth added as she and John sat on a settee nearby.

"Thank you, Mother," Mandie replied as she pushed back her long blond hair, which she had left hanging loose with a ribbon around it. "You look pretty yourself. You always do. And Grandmother looks as though she stepped out of a band box, like usual."

Mrs. Taft smiled at Mandie and turned to Elizabeth to ask, "Just when are the Woodards due in?"

"Sometime tomorrow afternoon," Elizabeth replied. Then she turned to Mandie and said, "You and I could go shopping in the morning before they get here if you'd like?"

"That would work out well because when Joe gets here, he and Amanda and I will go find a tree, and then tomorrow night we could all decorate it," John Shaw said, smiling at Mandie.

Mandie hesitated slightly before she said, "Well, yes, we could do that."

"And I suppose Uncle Ned, and possibly his family, will be coming to visit sometime during the holidays," Mrs. Taft said.

"Oh yes," Elizabeth began, "not only Uncle Ned but also—"

Mandie quickly interrupted as she asked, "Mother, I need to buy a present for Sallie. Maybe you could help me decide on something."

Uncle Ned was Mandie's father's old Cherokee friend, and Sallie was Ned's granddaughter. When Jim Shaw died the year before, the old man had promised that he would watch over Mandie, and Uncle Ned had kept his promise. No matter where Mandie traveled, he followed, all the way to Europe, to President McKinley's inauguration, to New York, or wherever.

Elizabeth frowned at having Mandie interrupt her, and before she could reply, Mandie noticed it and said quickly, "I'm sorry, Mother."

Her mother looked at her thoughtfully and said, "Let's not let that happen again. Now, I'll be glad to help you select a gift for Sallie when we go shopping tomorrow."

At that moment Liza appeared in the doorway to the hall and said, "Miz Lizbeth, de next-do' neighbors, dey be heah." She stepped aside, and Mrs. Cornwallis and Polly came into the room.

As soon as everyone exchanged greetings, Aunt Lou came to announce that supper was on the table, and they moved on into the dining room. Liza waited on the table under the watchful eye of Aunt Lou, who tended the sideboard.

"You got to leave school a day early," Mandie remarked to her neighbor, Polly, who was seated across the table from her.

"Yes," Polly replied, pushing back her long, dark hair as she gazed at Mandie with eyes as black as chinquapins.

"Well, did you go visit relatives?" Mandie asked as she ate her food. She wasn't really interested but was merely trying to make conversation.

"No," Polly said, picking up her cup of coffee.

"Did you come straight on home?" Mandie asked with a slight impatience at not being able to draw Polly into a conversation.

"No," Polly said, directing her gaze at the

adults, who were carrying on their own conversation.

Then Mandie realized Polly was listening to Uncle John because he was saying the Woodards would be in the next afternoon.

"I will be taking Amanda and Joe out to get a tree when they get here, so if you don't have one yet I'd be glad to bring in a tree for you," John Shaw was telling Mrs. Cornwallis.

Polly quickly intercepted with, "Mother, may I go with them? Please?"

Mrs. Cornwallis smiled her beautiful smile at her daughter and said, "But, Polly, you don't invite yourself."

"Of course she will be welcome to go with us," John Shaw immediately told the woman. "I just didn't think to ask if she wanted to."

"Oh, thank you, Mr. Shaw," Polly said excitedly.

"Yes, thank you, John," Mrs. Cornwallis said, smiling at him. "And we would like to invite y'all to come over and help us decorate it."

"Well, I don't know about that," John Shaw said, glancing at Elizabeth. "You see, we were making plans to decorate our tree tomorrow night, but both of you would be welcome to join in with us."

"That's no problem, John," Elizabeth spoke up. "We could put ours up tomorrow night, and since the next day is Sunday, we could do theirs after church in the afternoon." Looking at Mrs. Cornwallis, she added, "That is, if you would like to do that."

"That's fine," Mrs. Cornwallis said. "We'll just plan on that."

"What time tomorrow night are y'all going to put your tree up? In other words, what time do you want us to come over?" Polly asked excitedly.

Mrs. Taft joined in the conversation as she glanced at Mandie. "Don't forget, Elizabeth, that we have several other things we need to do tomorrow."

Mandie instantly understood what her grand-mother was aiming at. She was trying to prevent their evening from being taken up with Polly. Al-though Mrs. Taft was old, she was aware of the fact that Polly could be a nuisance when Joe came to visit. Mandie beamed a smile at her grandmother, who returned it.

"We will probably be all settled down to start decorating around eight o'clock, don't you sup-pose, John?" Elizabeth asked.

"That sounds about right," John agreed.

"Then Polly and I will come over about eight o'clock tomorrow night," Mrs. Cornwallis said.

Polly looked at John Shaw and asked, "But you will let me know when the Woodards get here and what time you're going after the trees, won't you, Mr. Shaw?"

John Shaw smiled at her and said, "I certainly will, Miss Polly, just as soon as they arrive."

Mandie drew a deep breath and looked up just in time to see Liza, who was standing behind Polly, make some kind of signs with her eyes and her hands. Mandie quickly figured out that Liza was tell-ing her to meet her in the kitchen later. She smiled and nodded at the girl, causing Polly to turn and look behind her as the young maid quickly moved across the room. Then Polly looked at Mandie but didn't say anything.

And evidently Aunt Lou had seen the exchange as she spoke loudly to Liza, "Git a move on, girl. Go git dem hot biscuits outa de oven."

Liza quickly left the room, and Aunt Lou started refilling everyone's coffee cups. Mandie couldn't imagine what was so secretive, or why Liza wanted her to come to the kitchen later. But she planned to do so at the very first moment she could slip away from everyone after they went back to the parlor.

After a while they were all settled down back in the parlor. Then Mandie suddenly remembered she had left Snowball in her room but couldn't recall if she had left the door open so he could come out. He needed to go to the kitchen to get his supper.

During a lull in the conversation, Mandie quickly stood up and said, "Mother, please excuse me, but I have to see if I left my door open so Snowball can come down and eat. I'll be right back."

"Yes, dear," Elizabeth replied, and the adults went on with their conversation.

"Polly, I'll only be a minute," Mandie promised as she hurriedly left Polly sitting on the settee in the parlor.

Racing up the steps, Mandie ran down the upstairs hallway and found her door closed. Opening it and going inside, she saw that Snowball was still on her bed but was now sitting up and washing himself.

"Oh, Snowball, I'm sorry. I left you shut up in here," Mandie told the cat as she gave him a little push off the bed. "Come on. It's time for you to eat."

The white cat shot out the door ahead of her, and Mandie quickly followed him to the kitchen. There were two places he always went—to her room to sleep and to the kitchen to eat. Mandie pushed open the door and let him in.

The servants had finished their supper and were

sitting at the long table drinking coffee. Snowball rushed to the bowl of food that had been placed under the cookstove for him.

"De comp'ny dun gone home?" Liza asked as she got up and went over to the sink.

"No, not yet," Mandie replied as she followed the girl across the room.

"Here," Liza said, holding up a piece of fried chicken. "I saved dis jes' fo' dat white cat, and I dun took de bones out of it." She offered it to Mandie.

Mandie didn't want to get her hands greasy because she had to return to the parlor. "You saved it, so you give it to him," she said.

Liza smiled at her and took the piece of chicken over to where Snowball was eating. She stooped down beside him and dangled the piece of meat. The cat immediately began meowing loudly and tried to snatch it from her fingers.

Mandie stooped down beside Liza and asked in a whisper, "What did you want me to come to the kitchen for?"

Liza dropped the piece of chicken in the cat's bowl and stood up. Mandie rose beside her.

"I heerd dat Miss Sweet Thing invitin' herself to come over when de doctuh son come tomorrow," Liza whispered back. "And I knows how to git rid of huh."

Mandie looked at the girl and asked, "Get rid of her? What do you mean?"

"I knows how to git rid of huh so's she don't come over heah ev'ytime de doctuh son come," Liza whispered. "I knows how."

"Liza, what are you talking about?" Mandie asked. "Hurry and tell me. I have to go back to the parlor before someone comes looking for me." She glanced at the other servants, who were carrying on their own conversation at the table.

The young girl moved closer to Mandie and whispered in her ear, "I knows how to put de spell on huh."

"Spell?" Mandie asked in a squeaky voice. She couldn't believe Liza had said that word.

"Voodoo," Liza whispered so low Mandie could barely hear her.

"Voodoo? Liza! That's witchcraft!" Mandie gasped in disbelief.

Liza vigorously shook her head. "Ain't neither!" she said. " 'Coordin' to dat Miss Sweet Thing's cook, voodoo be religion of all dem dead people whut lived befo' I got born, dem Africa people."

"Oh, Liza, forget about that," Mandie said. "We'd get in trouble all kinds of ways messing in that." She turned to leave the room.

Liza laid her hand on Mandie's arm to stop her. "Won't hurt nuthin' if we try it and see if it work," she said.

"No, Liza, we can't do that," Mandie said, pulling free and going toward the door.

Liza followed her and asked, "Why?"

Mandie stopped and stomped her foot, losing patience with the girl. "Because the devil might get us," she said. As she rushed on through the door, she heard Aunt Lou ask, "Liza, whut you done?"

When Mandie entered the parlor, she looked around the room but didn't see Polly. Her mother and Mrs. Cornwallis were talking, and Mandie went toward her grandmother and asked, "Where's Polly?"

"Why, dear, as soon as you left the room Polly jumped up and said she was going with you. Did you not see her?" Mrs. Taft asked.

Mandie puckered her lips and shook her head. "I'll go look for her," she said with a big sigh as she turned to leave the room. Then stopping to look back, she said to Mrs. Taft, "If she comes back, tell her to wait here for me please."

"I'll do that," her grandmother agreed.

Once out of the hearing of the people in the parlor, Mandie shook her head and began muttering to herself, "Now, where in the world did she go?"

Mandie quickly searched the downstairs of the big house, but Polly was not in any of the rooms. She hurried up to the second floor and went straight to her room to be sure Polly wasn't in there, and she wasn't. Firmly closing her door, Mandie started looking through the rest of that floor. Everything was quiet and the rooms were empty.

"She has to be somewhere," Mandie said to herself as she stood at the end of the hallway. "Where did she go?" She thought about it for a moment and then went down the back stairs to the kitchen.

"Has anybody seen Polly?" Mandie asked as she held the door half open and looked into the kitchen where the servants were cleaning up.

They all shook their heads no. Then Liza, stopping on her way to the sink, looked at Mandie and asked, "Dat Miss Sweet Thing's done disappeared? It sho' worked fast, didn't it?" She grinned.

"Liza, Grandmother said Polly followed me when I went up to get Snowball and brought him down here a while ago," Mandie explained. "Polly hasn't disappeared. I just can't find her."

"Same thang," Liza replied and continued to the sink with the load of dirty dishes she was carrying. She looked at Mandie and grinned again.

Mandie closed the door and walked down the hallway. She stopped to look in each room as she went, but everything was empty and quiet. Finally, she came to the doorway of the parlor. She looked inside and was amazed to see Polly sitting on the settee where she had left her when she went to get Snowball.

"Well, where did you go?" Mandie asked as she quickly entered the room and sat down beside the dark-haired girl.

"Go?" Polly repeated and then said, "Why, I went looking for you. Where did you go?"

Mandie took a deep, exasperated breath and said, "I went to my room, got Snowball, and took him down to the kitchen to eat his supper. That's where I went. And I have looked everywhere for you because Grandmother said you said that you were going after me. So where did you go?"

Polly shrugged and said, "Nowhere really. I came back because I couldn't find you."

"Did you go to the kitchen?" Mandie asked, remembering the conversation she had with Liza and wondering if Polly could have somehow overheard it.

"Goodness, no," Polly said. "Why would I go to the kitchen?"

"Because I went to the kitchen," Mandie replied with a deep breath. She looked at Polly, but evidently the girl had said all she was going to say.

Suddenly Mandie was aware that her mother was discussing plans for the holidays. "So you see, we are going to have a houseful with all these people coming to visit. In fact, we've asked Mr. and Mrs. Burns to come and help out," Elizabeth said.

"Burns? Oh, you mean the people who live in

John's tenant house," Mrs. Cornwallis replied.

"Yes, they are a great help in more ways than one," Elizabeth said.

Mandie quickly looked at her grandmother. She didn't seem to be upset, so maybe her mother had not named the Guyers in the list of expected guests.

"We are only expecting my sister and her daughter," Mrs. Cornwallis replied. "They probably won't get here until Monday, and Christmas is on Wednesday, so it won't be a long visit." She stood up and the others also rose. "But right now we must be getting home and let Mrs. Taft and Amanda rest after the journey from the school today. Thank you for inviting us."

Mandie breathed a sigh of relief. At last Polly was going home. Now maybe she would get a chance to talk to her grandmother about the Guyers. And maybe she could find out from her mother or Uncle John when they were expected to arrive.

As soon as Mrs. Cornwallis and Polly left, Mrs. Taft yawned and said, "I really am glad it's finally time to go to bed. It has been a long day."

They were all standing in the hallway after John Shaw had closed the door behind the Cornwallises.

"Grandmother, remember I wanted to speak to you for a minute," Mandie reminded the woman.

"Oh, I'm so sorry, Amanda, but I'm sure it can keep till the morrow. I'm just plain tuckered out," Mrs. Taft said as she started for the stairs.

Mandie turned back to her mother and Uncle John as they started to follow. "Mother, could I just ask you something, please?" she asked. She looked to be sure her grandmother had disappeared down the hallway.

"What is it, dear?" Elizabeth asked as they stood there.

"It's just that I don't know when the Guyers are coming, so I—"

"Oh, is that all? Well, neither does anyone else know," Elizabeth told her as she and Uncle John walked on toward the stairway with Mandie. "You know how busy Mr. Guyer stays with all that government business, and he wrote that they would be here but he was sorry he couldn't tell us when because of a special job he is doing."

"Oh shucks!" Mandie said. She quickly decided not to ask her mother if she had told her grandmother about their coming visit because she would have to tell her mother that for some reason Mrs. Taft didn't like Mr. Guyer.

At the top of the stairs they said good night and Mandie went to her room. Her door was standing open and Snowball was asleep in the middle of her bed. She distinctly remembered closing her door when she had gone looking for Polly.

As she got ready for bed she wondered whether Polly had been in her room. Or where had Polly gone?

And then there was the question of whether her grandmother knew the Guyers were coming.

And then there was the question of when the Guyers would arrive.

And probably the most important part of this whole thing was—what was going to happen with Joe and Jonathan in the same house for several days?

Mandie tossed and turned in bed a long time before she dropped off to sleep.

Chapter 3 / A Mysterious Package

The next morning Mandie opened her eyes to find Liza building a fire in the fireplace across the room. She stretched and sat up, almost sitting on her cat as she did. Snowball meowed angrily and jumped down to the floor. Liza looked up from the hearth.

"Lawsy mercy, Missy 'Manda, you 'bout kilt dat white cat," Liza said. Snowball came directly to her, sat down on the warm marble hearth, and began washing one of his front paws.

Mandie laughed, jumped out of bed, and went to the hearth to join her. "I didn't hurt him," she said. "He doesn't like it because I woke him up." She reached to pat Snowball's head, and he immediately backed away from her.

Liza laughed and said, "He sho' is mad wid you." She stood up and said, "Gotta go now, light up Miz Gramma's fire. Done 'em all but huhs."

"Is everybody up?" Mandie asked.

Liza shook her head and replied, "Ain't nobody up. I jes' startin' early 'cause all dat comp'ny comin'." She walked toward the door and then stopped to look back. "Where dat Miss Sweet Thing go last night when you couldn't find huh?"

"I don't know, Liza. She wouldn't tell me. She just said she went looking for me," Mandie explained.

"I jes' knows, dat I do," Liza said, laughing and dancing around the room. "I jes' knows."

Mandie stood up, put her hands on her hips, and asked, "And what do you know?"

"I knows dat spell work. Made dat Miss Sweet Thing plumb disappear," Liza replied, grinning at Mandie.

"Spell? Oh, Liza, that's all a bunch of nonsense," Mandie protested. "There is no such thing, and you'd better not let anyone hear you talking like that or you'll be in a heap of trouble."

"You jes' don't know 'bout spells. Dey works," Liza replied. She went to the door and opened it. Snowball whisked by her feet and disappeared into the hallway. "Dat white cat he be hungry. I go feed him soon as I light up Miz Gramma's fire." She stepped out into the hallway and closed the door.

Mandie shrugged her shoulders and said to herself, "Humph! Spells! No such thing!"

She brought her clothes over to the fireplace and dressed in the warmth from the fire, wondering how it would be waking up in a room heated by a furnace. While she was sure it would be much more comfortable, she loved the smell of wood burning and the sound of crackling as it fell into pieces. But she knew if she got too close she would practically scorch on whatever side of her was facing the fire, and then she would have to turn around and warm the other side.

"Anyhow, we will probably have all the furnaces in the schoolhouse when we go back after Christmas," she said to herself as she sat on the rug and buttoned her high-top shoes.

When Mandie was dressed, she went downstairs, intending to go to the kitchen and get a cup of hot coffee that the servants would have already made. But as she was about to pass the section of the hallway that went to the front door, she saw Snowball sitting there meowing, evidently wanting out.

"Snowball, you must have eaten awfully fast if Liza took you to the kitchen," Mandie told him. "But then, come to think of it, she said she had to go to Grandmother's room to start her fire, so you probably just ran off. Oh well, if you want out I'll open the door."

Mandie opened the heavy door enough to allow Snowball to slip through and was about to close it when she thought she saw something on the porch. Pushing the door open wider she saw what looked like a red box sitting on the top step.

"Well, what is that?" she said to herself. She pushed the screen door open and stepped out onto the porch. It was a large box wrapped with red paper. Mandie picked it up. It was a little heavy. She looked at a Christmas tag on the white ribbon. "Amanda Shaw!" she read out loud. "Wherever did this come from? I wonder who sent it?"

She hurried back inside the house, pushed the door shut with her foot, and ran into the parlor, where she placed the box on a table. She examined it again. Her name was written in rough block letters as though someone who could not write very well had written it. "Oh, what should I do?" she asked herself aloud.

"Open it, Missy 'Manda," Liza said from behind her.

Mandie had not heard the girl come into the room. "Do you know where this came from, Liza? I found it outside on the steps. It has my name on it."

Liza danced around the room without looking at her as she said, "Open it, Missy 'Manda."

Mandie frowned at the girl and began untying the ribbon. When she pulled off the red paper, she found a plain white box. She paused as she looked at it.

"Open de box, Missy 'Manda," Liza insisted as she came closer.

Mandie removed the lid and gazed at the contents in disappointment. "Why, Liza, it's nothing but a bunch of weeds and dirt, holly berries, and stuff," she said. She glanced at the girl who was also staring into the box.

Liza straightened up, smiled, and said, "But it sho' be a purty mess o' dirt, all dem red berries and holly leaves. Sho' look purty to me."

Mandie became suspicious of the girl. "Liza, did you send this to me?" she asked as she watched Liza.

Liza looked back down into the box and said, "Now, Missy 'Manda, whut fo' I go and send all dis heah stuff to you?"

"Do you know who did? Did you see anyone leave it on the doorstep?" Mandie asked.

Liza started across the room toward the door to the hall. "I gots to go," she said.

"Liza, what were you doing down at this end of

the hall? I thought you were helping in the kitchen," Mandie asked.

"I is," Liza replied. "I fed dat white cat, and he dun run 'way 'fo he finish de food. Aunt Lou she say bring him back to eat de rest, and I ain't found him yet."

"Well, he's outside, Liza," Mandie told her. "I just let him out the front door. That's how I found this box."

"Den I goes back to de kitchen," Liza said, hurrying out into the hallway and disappearing.

"And I'll just leave this silly present here," Mandie said, dropping the lid halfway back over the box and brushing her hands. "And I'll also go to the kitchen where I started in the first place and get me a cup of coffee."

When Mandie opened the kitchen door, she expected to find Liza telling Aunt Lou and Jenny about the gift. She was surprised to see the girl silently taking dishes down from the cupboard.

Aunt Lou closed the oven door, wiped her hands on her big white apron, and smiled at Mandie as she said, "And how's my chile this bright sunshiny mawnin'?"

"I'll be fine if I can beat you out of a cup of that coffee I smell perking away over there on the stove," Mandie replied with a big grin as she walked toward the stove.

"Dat won't be hard to do," Jenny said, reaching for a cup from the dishes Liza was setting down on the table. She filled it with coffee from the pot and set it on the table.

Mandie hurried to the icebox, took out the milk, and went to pour a little of it into her coffee. Then she added a little sugar from the bowl on the table.

Taking a sip from the cup, she looked at everyone and said, "Y'all make the best coffee I've ever tasted. I wonder what makes it so good?"

Aunt Lou and Jenny looked at each other. Liza stood by listening. When neither woman answered, the girl said quickly, "Dey puts black 'lasses in de coffee, dats whut dey do."

"Black molasses? In the coffee?" Mandie asked in surprise. Looking at Aunt Lou and Jenny, she asked, "Do y'all really put black molasses in the coffee?"

Aunt Lou laughed and said, "Dat be old-time secret, and Liza dun went and told. My mama and her mama befo' huh always put jes' a drop or two of good black molasses in de coffee. Takes out de bittuh taste."

"I won't tell anyone y'all's secret," Mandie promised as she sat down at the long table. "But I want to tell y'all about what was supposed to be a Christmas present to me." She explained about finding the gift-wrapped box on the front step. "I left it on the table in the parlor. When y'all have time, go and look at it. See what y'all think it is."

"I'll sho' do dat," Aunt Lou said as she turned back to open the oven.

"Sounds strange to me," Jenny said, getting another pot down from a hook on the wall.

"I dun seen it, and it do look strange," Liza said as she continued stacking dishes on the other end of the table.

"Thank you for the coffee," Mandie said as she took the last sip from her cup and stood up. "I'd better go and see if anyone else is up yet."

Aunt Lou looked at the clock ticking away on the shelf over the sink. "We be puttin' de food on de sideboard in de dinin' room in 'bout twenty minutes, you hear?"

"Yes, ma'am," Mandie replied as she left the room. "I'll tell everybody."

When she got back to the parlor, Mandie found her mother, Uncle John, and her grandmother studying the box she had left on the table. They all turned to look at her when she entered the room.

"What is this mess, Amanda?" her grandmother asked.

"I see your name here. Did someone actually send you this?" her mother asked.

"Doesn't make sense to me," Uncle John added.

"I don't know what it is, either, unless someone is trying to play a joke on me," Mandie replied, then she told them how she had found it. "Liza acted strange and wouldn't exactly answer my questions about it, so I'm a little suspicious of her."

"Would Liza do something like this?" Uncle John asked.

"Maybe she had good intentions. Maybe she wanted to give me a present and decided to make one herself. I suppose you could consider it a little garden of some sort," Mandie said, looking down at the contents of the box.

"It does look like something she would make," Mrs. Taft agreed.

"Well, maybe," Elizabeth said with doubt in her voice. "What are you going to do with it?"

"I thought after we put up the tree tonight I'll just set it under there," Mandie said. "The grass and leaves will dry up and wither away in a day or two anyhow."

"That's the best thing to do," her grandmother

agreed. "Then, if she did make this, it won't hurt her feelings."

"Right now I wonder if breakfast is ready," John Shaw said.

"It should be by the time we get to the dining room," Mandie told him.

And it was, with Liza standing by to refill coffee cups. Everyone greeted the girl with a big smile as they began filling their plates with food from the sideboard, and Mandie knew they were all thinking of her present, supposedly from Liza.

As they ate their breakfast, Elizabeth and Mandie discussed shopping.

"We'll take the buggy," Elizabeth told Mandie. "And we should be on our way as soon as we finish here so we'll have plenty of time to look around in the stores."

Mandie was worried that the Guyers might just happen to arrive while they were gone and would not receive a warm welcome from her grandmother. "It won't take much time to buy what's on my list," she told her mother.

"I don't really have a lot to purchase, either, but I thought if we just looked around awhile we might see something else we wanted," Elizabeth told her as she buttered a biscuit.

Mandie looked at her grandmother and asked, "Don't you want to go with us, Grandmother? We might see something you would like to buy."

"No, no, dear," Mrs. Taft replied, setting down her coffee cup. "You just go on with your mother and enjoy shopping. I have lots to do here—presents to wrap and letters to write. In fact, it will be nice to be left alone so I can catch up a little."

Mandie sighed to herself. Her grandmother was

not going to be persuaded, so she would just have to hurry through her shopping and persuade her mother to return home as soon as they were finished.

Franklin was not a very big town, but during the holidays out-of-town craftsmen set up their wares around the courthouse, on sidewalks, in vacant lots, and wherever they could find space to pitch a tent or build a temporary shelter. Most of the people around the countryside came into town to shop on Saturdays, and Mandie realized it was Saturday—the only Saturday left before Christmas. So she was not surprised to see the hundreds of shoppers about the town.

Elizabeth helped Mandie select some writing paper and envelopes for Sallie. "I know this kind of thing is scarce out there where the Cherokee people live," Elizabeth said as they looked at the supply in the stationer's shop.

"That is a good idea, Mother," Mandie agreed. "Sallie has mentioned having to write on just any kind of paper she can find. I know she'll like it."

Mandie quickly bought gifts for the other people left on her list—a wool scarf for Uncle John, a silk scarf for her grandmother, and a whole assortment of fancy hair clasps and combs for Celia. She and Celia had agreed to wait until they returned to school to exchange presents.

"I think I'll just buy wool gloves for Aunt Lou, Jenny, and Liza, and Abraham, too," Mandie said as they walked through an outdoor stall where a woman was selling handmade gloves and scarves and hats.

"That's a practical idea," Elizabeth told her. "Then I will get all of them scarves, and your uncle

John will, of course, be giving them extra pay for Christmas."

As Mandie selected the gloves and paid for them, Elizabeth purchased the scarves.

"Now I'm all finished," Mandie said. "I've already bought other presents in Asheville that I brought home in my trunk."

"Don't you want to walk around the block and see the rest of the goods these people are selling? We have plenty of time," Elizabeth said.

"Well . . ." Mandie said slowly as she tried to think of an excuse to go home. "I do have to wrap a lot of presents before the Woodards get here so I can put them under the tree tonight."

"All right, we'll go on back, then," Elizabeth agreed.

Since they lived within the town limits, it was only a short trip, but Mandie practically held her breath all the way, hoping the Guyers had not arrived. As soon as they entered the front hallway, she looked around anxiously. There was no one in sight. Then she saw Liza come out of the parlor.

"Has anyone else arrived yet, Liza?" Mandie asked as her mother went on toward the staircase, carrying her purchases.

"Nobody," Liza replied, stopping to look at Mandie. "Whut you buy?"

Mandie hugged her packages against her, smiled, and said, "I can't tell you. I have to go wrap everything." She started on down the hallway, looking back to be sure Liza was not following. "Is Grandmother in her room?"

"Nope, she dun went out soon as y'all left," Liza said.

"Who did she go with? Uncle John?" Mandie

asked as she stopped walking.

"Nope," Liza replied. "Some rich lady come knockin' at de do' and yo' gramma know huh. She went somewhere wid de lady in huh fancy buggy."

"You don't know who the lady was, Liza?" Mandie asked as she puzzled over this information.

"Nope," Liza said, and then with a big grin she added, "Missy 'Manda, don't you 'member how yo' gramma always likes to go out when y'all leaves huh heah alone? She's done dat befo'. 'Member?"

Now that Liza mentioned it, Mandie did remember her grandmother going out after everyone else left her alone in the house one time before. "I believe it was during Christmastime last year," she said thoughtfully. "Oh well, she probably just wanted to go shopping with her friend, whoever the woman was, Liza. Anyhow, I'm going to get these gifts all wrapped up before Joe comes."

She hurried upstairs to her room and deposited her packages on the bed. Quickly removing her gloves, she stuck them in the pockets of her coat. Then, taking off her hat and coat, she hung them in the wardrobe. "Brrrr!" she said to herself as she rubbed her hands together and walked toward the fireplace. "It's cold in here." She picked up the poker and pushed at the stack of burning logs with it. The flames went higher, and she put the poker back in its stand.

Mandie glanced at the packages and said, "Might as well get busy."

But as she was wrapping and tying ribbons, she thought about her grandmother. She really should get her to stay still long enough to explain to her that the Guyers were coming for the holidays. So far Mrs. Taft had been too busy and put her off, but

Mandie just had to tell her. Otherwise, if the Guyers came walking in and Mrs. Taft had not been told, she would be awfully angry with Mandie. But if Mandie could have a few minutes to explain things to her, maybe she wouldn't be too upset.

Suddenly Mandie realized she had been so deep in thought she didn't remember what was in each package that she had wrapped.

"Oh shucks! Now I'll have to unwrap them to see what belongs to whom," she said. "Then I'll have to wrap them all up again. Double work!"

Mandie was careful this time to mark the packages as she rewrapped everything. And finally she was finished.

"Now I'll just go downstairs and wait for Grandmother to return. I'll catch her as soon as she comes in the front door," Mandie said aloud to herself.

Chapter 4 / Visitors

When Mandie got down to the parlor, she found her mother and Uncle John already there.

"Has Grandmother come back yet? You know she went out as soon as we left?" Mandie asked her mother as she sat down on a chair near her.

"No, dear, she won't return until sometime this afternoon. She left me a note," Elizabeth explained. "Mrs. Willimon, an old friend of hers, heard that Mother was here and came by. They'll be having the noon meal at her house, so whenever Aunt Lou has ours ready, we'll go ahead and eat."

"But Grandmother told us she has so much to do she couldn't go shopping with us," Mandie reminded her.

"Evidently Mrs. Willimon's visit was unexpected," Elizabeth replied.

"Oh, you know how your grandmother is anyway," Uncle John said with a smile. "Just whatever whim strikes her, that's what she does."

Mandie was beginning to believe that her grandmother was deliberately avoiding talking with her,
and she couldn't figure out why. Maybe Mrs. Taft
thought Mandie just wanted to discuss some trivial
matter. But on the other hand, maybe she believed
Mandie wanted to discuss some troubling matter
that she didn't especially want to hear about. But no
matter what, Mandie was determined to get a
chance to tell her about the Guyers' coming visit.

A few minutes later Aunt Lou came to the parlor
door to announce, "Miz 'Lizbeth, de food be on de
table."

"Thank you, Aunt Lou," Elizabeth said as she
and John stood up.

Mandie rose and followed them to the door but
suddenly ran ahead into the hallway as the knocker
on the front door sounded. "It's probably the Woodards," she called back to her mother.

When she opened the heavy door with stained-
glass panels, she did find the Woodards on the
porch. Elizabeth and John came to welcome them.

Mandie waited for Joe to enter behind his parents. "Oh, Joe, you've just got to see the strangest
present I ever received. Come to the parlor," Mandie told him as she started back toward the parlor.

"Amanda," Elizabeth stopped her. "That can
wait until later. I'm sure the Woodards all want to
freshen up, and then we'll eat before the food gets
cold."

"Yes, ma'am," Mandie replied as she realized
her mother was right.

Aunt Lou had stayed in the hallway, and now she
started toward the kitchen as she called back, "I'll
go git mo' plates on de table, Miz 'Lizbeth." She
went on her way.

"I hope we are not interrupting your meal," Mrs. Woodard said.

"Oh no, you're just in time, in fact, and I'm glad because we weren't sure exactly when you all would get here," Elizabeth said as she walked toward the staircase and led the way upstairs. "Come on. I'll show you your rooms."

As they all went up the steps, Mandie waited in the downstairs hallway. Joe called back to her, "We won't be long."

They weren't very long, but they all came back down together and went directly to the dining room. Mandie would have to wait to show the gift to Joe.

Once they had all been served, Dr. Woodard spoke from across the table, "And how are you, Miss Amanda?"

"Fine, Dr. Woodard," Mandie replied. "Has Mr. Jacob Smith moved into my father's house yet like he promised?"

"Why, yes, he did move in a week or two after y'all got all that settled in court and you asked him to take care of it," Dr. Woodard replied as he cut the piece of ham on his plate. "And he has certainly been taking care of it. Sure looks like a different place. He has painted everything and has cleared the overgrown fields and plans to start farming the land."

Mandie smiled with satisfaction. "I knew he would fix everything up because he was my father's friend," she said. "And I'm so glad we found him when we needed to clear up my father's will."

Mandie had lived in a log cabin at Charley Gap near the Woodards until her father died, then she had come to stay with her uncle John Shaw who had married her mother later.

"And did you and your friend Celia Hamilton and her mother get home all right from that exciting trip to New York?" Joe asked, setting down his coffee cup.

New York! Oh, my goodness, Mandie remembered. *Joe doesn't know that the Guyers are coming!* She quickly cleared her throat and said, "Oh yes, we had a nice trip home on the train. Did you find a college up there that you might want to attend?"

"I don't think so," Joe said, shaking his head, causing a lock of brown hair to fall forward on his brow. "New York is too big, and there are too many people up there to suit me."

John Shaw joined in the conversation and turned to ask Dr. Woodard, "Where else will you be looking for a college for Joe?"

"Well, there are several places," Dr. Woodard replied. "We're hoping Joe won't want to go too far off so he can come home now and then."

"Yes," Mrs. Woodard agreed. "The house will feel awfully empty without Joe around and Dr. Woodard gone so much on patient visits."

"Oh, Mom, you can come to college and visit me," Joe said with a big teasing grin.

"I know how you feel," Elizabeth said to Mrs. Woodard. "With Amanda away in school in Asheville, I don't see a whole lot of her, but it's all for her good, to get a good education. She'll inherit a lot of business problems someday."

Dr. Woodard laughed and said, "I don't think I'd exactly call it business problems. To me it's more like a lot of business money."

"But you can't have money without having problems, too," John Shaw said.

"Yes, you're right, of course," Dr. Woodard said, looking around the table. "Did Mrs. Taft not come with Amanda?"

"She came, but she's out visiting with friends right now," Elizabeth said.

Mandie wondered how she would ever talk to her grandmother alone now that the Woodards had arrived. She glanced at Joe and thought about breaking the news to him that Jonathan was coming. She was sure the two boys would try to outdo each other the whole time they were there. And come to think of it, she realized she was not even sure she had told Jonathan that Joe and his family would also be staying at her house for the holidays. Oh, what a mess she had caused for herself. Uncle Ned, her father's old Cherokee friend, had always told her to "think first, then act," and she had an awful time remembering to do that.

"Mandie," Joe said sharply, bringing her back to the present. "What are you dreaming about?"

"Oh, I'm sorry, Joe," Mandie said, flustered with being caught in her thoughts.

"Must have been something awful the way you were frowning," Joe teased.

"It was," Mandie agreed with a nervous laugh.

"How awful?" Joe asked, grinning at her.

"Shall we go into the parlor for coffee?" Elizabeth was saying at the end of the table.

Mandie drew a sigh of relief upon being saved from further explanation. She realized everyone was finished with the meal, and her mother was rising to lead the way back to the parlor.

"Come on," she told Joe as the two stood up and followed the adults. "I want to show you that strange present I mentioned."

When they entered the parlor, Mandie edged around the adults and went straight to the box sitting on the table where she had left it. Joe followed.

"Look at this mess that someone wrapped up, put my name on, and left on the doorstep. I found it early this morning," Mandie explained as she pulled the gift wrapping back for a full view.

Dr. and Mrs. Woodard glanced at it as they walked past to sit near the fireplace.

"Some child must have made all that," Dr. Woodard said.

"Unless it was meant to be a joke," Mrs. Woodard added as they sat down.

Joe bent over the box to inspect the contents. He turned this way and that, mumbled under his breath, and then straightened up with a serious look on his face to announce, "Looks like a treasure map to me."

"A treasure map?" Mandie quickly asked. She bent closer to look. "Why, yes, it could be a treasure map. Now, why didn't I think of that?"

"Oh, Mandie, I was only joking," Joe said with a little laugh. "I know how much you love mysteries."

Mandie continued gazing at the twigs, berries, and dirt. "But look, Joe," she said, pointing to some twigs tied with bits of red ribbon. "Those could be markers on the road to some hidden treasure. And these little dents in the dirt could be roads. See?" She glanced at Joe.

"Might be, but I doubt it," he said. "Looks more like a jumble of holly leaves and berries and dirt, all just thrown into the box and patted down."

"But, Joe, all this must mean something," Mandie argued as she straightened up to look at him.

"Somebody sent it to me for some reason."

"Probably some young child," Joe said.

"But I don't know any child who would do this," Mandie said thoughtfully, trying to remember just how many children she knew in Franklin. "In fact, I don't know any children anywhere near here. And they would have to live close by in order to bring this box and leave it on our doorstep at night. No, I'm sure it's a treasure map, just like you said."

"And I think I said the wrong thing. Look, Mandie, I was only joking," Joe replied, waving his hands at the box. "Why, you could never make any sense out of that mess to try and follow it as a map."

"We could try," Mandie insisted.

Uncle John spoke from across the room. "Are you two ready to go bring in a Christmas tree?" he asked.

"Oh yes," Mandie agreed and explained to Joe, "Polly Cornwallis invited herself to go with us."

"Well, well!" Joe said with a big sigh.

"Uncle John, should we go get Polly now?" Mandie asked as her uncle rose from his chair.

"Why don't you ask Liza to run over and let her know we are ready to go while we go get our coats?" John Shaw replied. "Ask Liza to tell her we'll be in the barn. I have to get the ax and some rope."

"All right," Mandie agreed as she left the room and went to the kitchen.

She found Liza stacking dirty dishes in the sink while Aunt Lou and Jenny brought everything in from the dining room table.

"Liza, Uncle John said to ask you to let Polly know we are ready to go get the trees and for her to meet us in the barn," Mandie said.

Liza stopped her work, put her hands on her hips, and said, "Dat Miss Sweet Thing sho' gwine git things poppin'. But don't you worry none, Missy 'Manda, 'cause she might disappear agin."

"Oh, Liza, please hurry," Mandie said impatiently. "And please tell Polly to hurry, too. As soon as we get these trees, Joe and I are going on a treasure hunt, but, of course, don't tell Polly that."

"I knows you wants huh to go back home when y'all gits de trees, but I heahs tell dat Miss Sweet Thing and huh mama gwine come over heah tonight to he'p fancy up de tree," Liza said.

"That's right, Liza. Uncle John asked them," Mandie replied.

"So when you and de doctuh son gwine on dis heah huntin' treasure? Where dis treasure be anyhow?" Liza asked as she stared at Mandie.

"I have no idea where the treasure is or what it might be. You saw that present I found on the doorstep this morning. Well, as soon as Joe saw it, he declared it was a treasure map," Mandie explained.

"Den how you gwine find it?" Liza asked.

"Oh, Liza, I've got to go up to my room and get my coat," Mandie said, turning to leave the kitchen. "Please hurry and tell Polly we're ready. Thank you." She smiled back at Liza as she quickly left the room.

Mandie rushed to her room, put on her hat, coat, and gloves, and hurried back downstairs and out to the barn to join Uncle John and Joe. As she came to the open door and looked inside the building, she couldn't believe what she was seeing. Polly Cornwallis was already there and was hovering around Joe, who was assisting John Shaw in taking the ax down from its rack. How did she get there so fast?

"I'm ready," Mandie announced from the door-way.

"So am I," Polly said as she turned to look at Mandie. "This is going to be exciting."

Mandie frowned and asked, "Exciting?"

"Oh yes," Polly began explaining. "Mr. Shaw said we're going to walk through his woods and pick out any tree we want, and I have decided exactly what kind of a tree I want for our house. It's got to be—"

"Let's get on our way now," John Shaw inter-rupted. "It looks like snow, and we want to get back before it starts." He went out the door with the ax over his shoulder.

Polly walked close to Joe as he carried the roll of rope and left the barn. Mandie stepped to his other side.

"Snow," Polly repeated. "I think it would be so delightful to scrunch along in the snow, don't you, Joe?"

Joe didn't even look at her as he said, "Not to-day."

The three young people followed John Shaw through his acres and acres of land until he came to the wooded area. Then he stopped, turned around, and said, "Beginning here look around and decide what you want for the house, Amanda, and, Polly, you choose one for yours."

Mandie quickly looked up at Joe and asked, "Will you help me find one that will reach the ceil-ing? I'm not sure how to judge the height."

"That won't be hard to do," Joe replied as he stepped ahead and pointed to the left. "All those trees in that cluster over there are more or less the right height."

"I'd say you're right," John Shaw agreed as he looked at the trees.

"Then the next thing I'd like is to have one that has thick limbs that fan out in graduated heights," Mandie explained as she walked through the group of trees.

"Well, what about mine? Aren't y'all going to help me find one?" Polly asked with a pout.

"Of course," John Shaw told her. "Just tell us what you want."

"I suppose whatever Mandie is getting will be all right for our house, too," Polly replied as she inspected the trees.

"Do you want pine or cedar, Mandie?" Joe asked as he and Mandie pushed their way through the thick growth of trees.

"Cedar. It smells so good," Mandie replied. She stopped to touch the limbs of a cedar. "This one looks about right, doesn't it?"

"I'd say so," Joe agreed. "Want me to cut that one down for you?"

"Please," Mandie replied with a big smile.

Joe took the ax from John Shaw and began chopping into the trunk of the cedar as he moved around it. Polly stopped her search to stand and watch with Mandie.

As the trunk was finally severed, Uncle John and Joe threw ropes around it and pulled it down from its tight fit between the other trees.

"Oh, it's going to be beautiful when we decorate it," Mandie exclaimed as she watched it fall to the ground.

"Now, Miss Polly, where's the one you want?" John Shaw asked.

"Let me look a minute," Polly said, wandering

through the trees. She stopped at one and said, "I believe this one is about right."

"Then we'll take it down," John Shaw said as he reached for the ax from Joe. He was about to land a blow on the trunk when she changed her mind.

"No, no, wait just a minute. I believe it's too skinny," Polly said as she moved on among the trees. "Maybe this one here." She looked up at the height. "No, I believe it's too tall."

"How about this one over here?" John Shaw asked, indicating a cedar almost identical to the one Mandie had chosen.

Polly looked at it, screwing up her mouth, and tossed back her long, dark hair. "I think it's too out of shape or something," she finally said and walked on.

Mandie, Joe, and John Shaw stood there watching and waiting for her to make a decision. And all at once a shower of snowflakes fell through the trees.

"Polly, please make your mind up. It's snowing. We have to go home," Mandie called to her as she wiped the snowflakes from her face.

Polly stopped to look upward and reached out her gloved hands for the flakes. "Oh, isn't it beautiful? I was hoping it would snow," she said.

"I'm sorry, Miss Polly, but we do have to be getting back to the house," John Shaw told her firmly.

Polly looked at his stern face and went directly back to the first tree she had selected and said, "Then I'll just take this one."

John Shaw quickly began swinging the ax before she changed her mind again, and no one spoke until the tree was swinging free.

"At last," Mandie said under her breath.

Uncle John and Joe attached the rope to the tree, and between the four of them they managed to carry the trees to the yard behind the Shaw house. The snowflakes became thicker and were fast covering everything in white.

"Let's just put ours on the back porch and run Polly's over to her house," John Shaw told Joe.

Polly hesitated and said, "I suppose I'd better go on home and show you where to put it. I was going to go in with you, Mandie, but I'll be back tonight with my mother." She started after John Shaw and Joe, who were already moving across the yard with the tree.

"All right, Polly," Mandie called to her as she went in the back door of the house. She stomped the snow from her feet and brushed the flakes from her coat and hat and gloves. She removed them and hung them on pegs by the back door in the hallway.

Liza opened the kitchen door and looked out into the hallway. "I be thinkin' I be hearin' sumpin' out heah," she said. "Where dat Miss Sweet Thing?"

Mandie laughed and said, "She went on home to show Uncle John and Joe where to put her tree. Ours is on the back porch. She said she'd be back tonight with her mother." Mandie went into the kitchen and straight to the warmth of the big iron cookstove.

"But she ain't a'comin' tonight," Liza said with a big grin. "Huh mama dun sent word. Got unexpected comp'ny. Cain't come." She laughed and danced around the room.

Mandie looked at her with a big smile and said, "You aren't joking, are you?"

"Nope, ain't comin'," Liza replied. "Told you I

could make huh disappear."

Mandie laughed and said, "But you didn't make her disappear. They have company, so they can't come over here because of that."

"But it's unexpected comp'ny," Liza reminded her.

Mandie suddenly remembered her white cat. She had not seen him since before the meal at noon. She looked around the room and asked, "Liza, do you know where Snowball is?"

"I sho' does, and I ain't tellin' nobody else," Liza said. Then she bent closer to Mandie and whispered, "He be on Miz Gramma's bed fast asleep."

"On Grandmother's bed! Oh, she won't like that. I'd better go and get him," Mandie said as she started to leave the kitchen.

"Wait! Ain't no hurry! Miz Gramma ain't come back home yet," Liza told her.

Mandie paused at the door and said, "So Grandmother is still out with Mrs. Willimon." And then she quickly added, "But it's snowing outside and she will probably be home any minute now, so I'd better get him out of her room."

She rushed out into the hallway and up the stairs. She didn't want to have her grandmother upset because she still had to tell her that the Guyers were coming to visit. And that was going to be enough to put Mrs. Taft in a bad mood.

Chapter 5 / Getting Ready

The door to Mrs. Taft's room was slightly ajar. Mandie quickly pushed it open and headed for the tall bed on the other side of the huge room.

"Snowball! Snowball!" she called as she went. "Come here. You know you aren't supposed to go in Grandmother's room. Snowball!" She looked on the counterpane, but her white cat was not there. She quickly searched the room and decided he was not there.

She left the bedroom, pulling the door shut behind her, and hurried down the long hallway toward her room. Halfway there she met her grandmother, who had just reached the top of the steps.

"Oh, Grandmother, I didn't know you were back," Mandie said nervously, hoping the lady had not seen her come out of her bedroom.

"I thought I'd better get back while the snow has stopped—just in case it starts again," Mrs. Taft said, removing her hat as she hurried on toward her room.

Mandie only heard the words that the snow had stopped, and she raced for the stairs. If she and Joe were going to try to decipher that treasure map, they'd better begin now. She met Joe at the bottom of the steps.

"The snow stopped," she said to him.

"I know. Mr. Shaw and I just got back from Polly's house, and there's hardly a trace of the white stuff outside now," Joe told her. He was carrying his coat and hat.

"But it might snow again, so let's get started with that treasure map," Mandie told him. "I'll get my coat and things. I left them in the back hallway." She started in that direction.

"Wait, Mandie!" Joe quickly said. As she stopped and turned around, he asked, "How are we going to figure out any treasure map from that mess in the box you received?"

"We'll have to study it real hard," Mandie said. She walked on. "I'll be right back."

She quickly got her coat and hat and put them on as she came back to where Joe was sitting on the bottom step.

"Let's go get the box and take it out on the porch," Mandie told him.

Joe followed her to the parlor where Elizabeth, John Shaw, and the Woodards were sitting by the fire. Mandie hurried over to the table, picked up the box, and said, "We're going outside."

"All right, dear, but don't go too far away. We may have more company coming, you know," Elizabeth told her.

Mandie gasped. Did her mother believe the Guyers were coming that afternoon? She and Joe would just have to stay within sight of the house so she could watch for them. "All right, Mother," she said as she and Joe left the parlor. Joe hurried to open the front door for Mandie. With her arms full of wrapping paper and the box, she was trying to hold it as level as possible so the contents would not be disturbed.

"Now, let's look this thing over real good," Mandie said. She sat down on the swing on the porch and Joe joined her. She set the box between them, removed the wrapping paper, and folded it, tucking it in the corner of the seat.

Joe bent forward to look at the contents. "I don't see a thing but a lot of dirt, weeds, holly leaves, berries, and some little red ribbons, Mandie," he said.

"But it all must mean something. Whoever made this must have had some idea as to what it is," Mandie said, frowning as she concentrated on the stuff. "I still think those little dents in the dirt represent roads and those red ribbons are landmarks along the way."

"If that's so, then where is the dead end, the place where the treasure should be?" Joe asked, looking at her.

Mandie thought for a moment and then looked out across the huge front yard. Signs of the snow were gone except for white powder here and there. "It's probably the last ribbon along the way," she said thoughtfully, looking back down at the contents of the box. "You see, if you went along one of the dents, or a road, you would pass two of the ribbons in order to get to the third ribbon."

"Then where do we begin?" Joe asked.

"Well, we can start right here," Mandie said,

picking up the box and going down the long walkway. "We walk down to the gate here. And that could be the first red ribbon." She stopped and looked around as Joe followed.

"All right, the road in front of your house here goes both ways," he said. "Do we go left or right?"

Mandie studied the contents of the box a moment and then said, "If we go left, we will come to the intersection of another road. But if we go right, we'll only keep going down the same road. Let's go left." She pushed open the gate and started down the road to the left.

"At least this is good exercise," Joe remarked as he walked along with her. "Tell me. What do you expect to find at the end of this treasure hunt?"

Mandie stopped to look up at him. "Why, Joe Woodard, that's the fun of going on a treasure hunt. You never know what you'll find. If you did, there wouldn't be any sense in going at all."

"I'd really like to know who sent you that box," Joe said, looking down at the contents. "That might just give us an inkling of what this is all about."

"So would I, but since we don't know, we can find out if we solve this mysterious treasure map," Mandie said.

When they came to the intersection, they stopped and looked around.

"Now which way do you plan to go?" Joe asked, looking at the box and then up and down the other road.

"Let's see. If this is the first red ribbon, then we should go right toward the next ribbon," Mandie said as she studied the contents.

Joe glanced back in the direction of the house. "I do believe I see Uncle Ned turning into your driveway in his wagon," he said.

Mandie quickly turned around to look. "Yes, that must be Uncle Ned, and he probably has Morning Star and Sallie with him because he's in the wagon. Come on. Let's go back." She held the box closely to her and hurried back down the road.

As they reached the front gate, the wagon disappeared around behind the house, and they followed it until it stopped in front of the barn. Mandie looked up and saw Uncle Ned as he stepped down. She glanced back up. There was no one with him.

"Uncle Ned," she greeted him. "I'm so glad you've come. I thought maybe Sallie and Morning Star would be with you since you're in the wagon."

The old Cherokee put his arm around her thin shoulders and said, "Not today. Three days I bring Sallie and Morning Star."

"Three days?" Mandie said, quickly counting in her head. "That would be Christmas Eve, which is Tuesday. Oh, I'm so glad y'all are coming for Christmas."

Uncle Ned turned to shake hands with Joe. "Glad to see you," he said.

"And I'm glad to see you, sir," Joe replied. "My mother and father are here, too."

"Well, come on. Let's go in the house," Mandie said, starting toward the back door, and then she stopped and held the box out for Uncle Ned to see. "Look at what somebody sent me, all wrapped up like a Christmas present, with no name on it. I found it on the doorstep this morning."

The old Indian glanced at the box, looked at Mandie, and asked, "What this be?"

"I've decided it must be a treasure map," Mandie declared and went on to explain about the dents and ribbons.

Uncle Ned shook his head as she finished. Smiling, he said, "No treasure. Mess."

"I think you're right, Uncle Ned," Joe told him.

Mandie stomped her foot and said, "Oh shucks! Let's go in the house." She led the way in through the back door, left the box on a table there, and began removing her coat, hat, and gloves as she went into the parlor.

"Welcome, Uncle Ned," John Shaw said as they entered the parlor, and he rose to shake hands.

Greetings were exchanged all around because everyone knew Uncle Ned. Mandie pulled up a stool near him when he sat down and waited to ask why he was alone in the wagon when he always rode his horse.

"I bring baskets, sell to store people for holiday," he said.

"Oh, Mother, we ought to go buy some of them Monday," Mandie said.

"Yes, we will," Elizabeth promised. "They will make nice presents to some of the people on our lists." Turning to the old Indian, she said, "I wish you had brought Morning Star and Sallie with you."

He explained that he would return with them on Christmas Eve.

"I hope you are planning to stay tonight with us before you start back over the mountain," John Shaw told him.

Uncle Ned smiled and nodded as he said, "Thank you. I stay. Leave sunup tomorrow."

"We just brought in a tree this afternoon, so you'll be here to help us decorate it," Mandie told him.

"And I'd appreciate it, Uncle Ned, if you could take our presents to everyone back your way," Elizabeth said.

"Yes, glad to," Uncle Ned replied.

Elizabeth looked at Mandie and asked, "Amanda, do you have all your gifts wrapped, the ones to the people who won't be able to come visit for Christmas?"

"Well, I have a few things in my trunk I brought home from school that I haven't wrapped," Mandie said.

"Why don't you go finish now while you have time? Uncle Ned will be leaving early in the morning," Elizabeth told her.

Mandie stood up, looked at Joe, and said, "It won't take long."

John Shaw rose and said to Joe, "We brought in the tree, but we still have to find some mistletoe and holly."

"Yes, sir, and I think I remember seeing a whole bunch of mistletoe on the way to the woods today," Joe said as he also stood up.

"I go along," Uncle Ned said.

"And I would like a little exercise myself," Dr. Woodard told him.

As the men and Joe left the room to hunt mistletoe and holly, Mandie looked back at her mother, her grandmother, and Mrs. Woodard in the parlor. "I won't be gone long," she said.

"All right, dear," Elizabeth replied.

Mandie hurried upstairs to her room. The minute she pushed open the door, she knew something was wrong. As she stepped into the room, she saw Snowball curled up asleep in the middle of her bed. And he was practically covered with the paper torn from the presents she had wrapped earlier.

"Snowball!" she cried as she ran toward the bed. "What have you done?" She quickly examined the gifts to see if he had clawed them. Nothing looked damaged, but she would have to finish pulling off the wrappings and do everything all over again.

"Oh, I could shake you good!" she declared as the white cat stood up, stretched, and jumped down from the bed. He took one look at his mistress and quickly ran out into the hallway. "You'd better stay out of here," she added as she went to close the door.

When she finished redoing the presents, she put them in the bottom of the huge wardrobe this time and closed the doors. Then she had to get the things out of her trunk that she had bought for some of her Cherokee kinpeople and wrap them. Uncle Ned would be taking these. She sat down at the desk in her room and wrote notes to each of the recipients, wishing them well and a glorious holiday.

"Now I need something to put all this in so Uncle Ned can carry the things back with him," Mandie said to herself.

She went to the linen closet in the hallway and searched through the stacks there. "If I can only find some flour sacks," she said to herself. "Ah, here are some." She pulled out a few sacks that were folded and tucked at the bottom of the stack. When she unfolded one, she was disappointed to see that someone had ripped out the seams. She knew the stitching in flour sacks was made with an end thread that if pulled would immediately unravel the whole seam. Evidently this had been done to these. She looked in other stacks in the closet and finally found three flour sacks that were still sewn in the seams.

Back in her room she quickly filled the bags with the wrapped presents and the notes she had written. The flour sacks were the large thirty-six-pound size, so she only had to use two. The third one she folded and put on her bureau. Then she gathered up the tops of the bags and looped them so the contents wouldn't spill out. She set them on a chair and made sure she closed the door when she left her room.

Mandie went back downstairs to the parlor and found everyone had returned and also that it was almost time for supper. Where did the time go?

"What took you so long, dear?" Elizabeth asked as Mandie sat down on a small settee beside Joe.

"That white cat had completely torn up the paper on the presents I had wrapped after we went shopping today, and I had to redo everything, plus all the things I had in my trunk," Mandie explained, pointing to Snowball, who was now curled up asleep on the carpet in front of the fireplace.

"Amanda, you need to start closing the door to your room when you go out so Snowball can't get in there," Mrs. Taft told her.

"I know, but I always forget, and he goes in and sleeps on my bed," Mandie said with a sigh. "But I'm sure I closed it this time."

"We've got the whole back porch full of holly and mistletoe," Joe told Mandie with a big grin. "You girls won't be able to find a safe place to stand away from the mistletoe."

Mandie smiled and said, "That's what you think. But come to think of it, Polly might like being caught under the mistletoe."

"The Cornwallises are not coming over tonight,

Amanda," Elizabeth said from across the room. "They have unexpected company."

"Oh, that's right. Liza told me," Mandie said. Turning to Uncle Ned, she said, "I have my presents all wrapped and ready in two flour sacks whenever you get ready to take them."

"In morning I will get," the old man said.

Aunt Lou came to the doorway at that moment and announced, "De food be on de table, Miz 'Lizbeth."

"Thank you, Aunt Lou. We'll be right in," Elizabeth said as she stood up.

They went into the dining room for supper, and afterwards they returned to the parlor to plan the decorating.

"I believe the first thing we need to do is get the pot for the tree out of the barn and get the tree standing," John Shaw said.

"The pot? Oh, you mean that same old bucket you use every year," Mandie said. "I know where it is. Joe and I could go get it." She looked at him, and he nodded.

"We'll bring it in and put it in place, and then we'll carry in dirt to fill it here. That way it won't be too heavy to carry, and the tree will stand up better," John Shaw said.

"Need ladder," Uncle Ned said. "I get ladder."

"And a hammer and some tacks. I know where they are," Elizabeth said.

"Well, if you'll just tell me where you keep the skirt for the bottom of the tree, I'll get it," Mrs. Taft said to Elizabeth.

"It's in the linen closet down the hall next to the kitchen door," Elizabeth replied.

"And Dr. Woodard and I can get the little ornaments, or whatever you plan to put on the tree, if you'll just tell us where they are," Mrs. Woodard said.

"Please wait, everybody! We are forgetting something," Mandie suddenly spoke up loudly as she stepped into the middle of the floor.

Everyone turned to look at her.

"What are we forgetting, Amanda?" Elizabeth asked.

"Don't you remember? A long time ago we agreed that all the servants would be asked to join in with us when we decorate the tree," Mandie reminded her.

"Oh yes," Elizabeth agreed.

"Thank you for reminding us. I don't know how I forgot that," John Shaw said. "Now, why don't you run back to the kitchen and round everybody up so we can get to work?"

Mandie rushed out of the room and came back with Aunt Lou and Liza. "Abraham and Jenny wanted to get the tree pot out of the barn," she explained. "They'll be here in a minute."

John Shaw looked around the room and said, "We're still forgetting Jake and Ludie Burns, and did Jason Bond get back from his visit over the mountain?"

"Why don't Mandie and I run down and get the Burnses?" Joe asked.

"All right. I thought they would have been here by now. They've agreed to help out in the house during the holidays," John Shaw said. "Has no one seen Jason Bond?"

Everyone shook their heads.

"Then he should be back soon," John Shaw said. Looking at Dr. Woodard, he added, "He always takes food and toys to the settlement of poor folks on the other side of the mountain. He has been gone all day, so he should return soon. Amanda, get your coat, then you and Joe run along and get the Burnses. Take a lantern. There's one on the back porch."

Aunt Lou and Liza stood at the doorway looking and listening. And Abraham and Jenny came in, carrying the huge pot.

"Whereabouts y'all be wantin' dis heah pot?" the old man asked.

"Just set it down right there, Abraham, and we'll figure out where," John Shaw told him.

As Abraham and Jenny set the pot down, Mandie started to go out the door to get her coat and hat. Joe followed. They almost ran straight into Polly Cornwallis.

"Well!" Mandie said in surprise. "I thought you weren't coming over tonight."

"Mother said I could because my aunt and uncle came to visit for the weekend and they're old," Polly said, wrinkling up her nose. "I didn't have anybody to talk to, so here I am."

"Well, go on in," Joe said, stepping out of her way and motioning her into the parlor. "Mr. Shaw is giving out work orders, so you might as well let him know you're here so you can get yours." He grinned at her.

"Work orders? What in the world for?" Polly asked in surprise.

"Everybody has a part in putting up the tree and decorating, so all you have to do is say what you want to do. Joe and I are going to get the Burnses," Mandie said, stepping past her to get her coat and hat where she had left them on the hall tree.

"You are? Then I'll just go with y'all," Polly said, turning to follow Mandie.

"We're going to walk real fast. We have to hurry," Mandie warned her.

"I can walk as fast as you can, Mandie Shaw," Polly said with a frown.

"Then let's get going," Joe told the girls as he put on his coat and cap. "Let's go out the back door so we can get the lantern."

Mandie went through the kitchen and picked up some matches and joined Joe and Polly on the back porch. Joe lit the lantern, and they were on their way. The winter day had been short because of cloudiness, and it was dark as the three hurried down the pathway.

When they reached the Burnses' house, they knocked on the front door and Mrs. Burns opened it, surprised at seeing them.

"Well, bless my soul, do come in," she told the young people. "I was just getting ready to go, as soon as Jake gets his things together." She stepped back so they could enter the small front room.

"Uncle John sent us after y'all," Mandie explained.

"I'm sorry you had to come all the way down here for us," she said. "You see, we didn't know exactly what time youins wanted us up there. Then when it started to snow today, we decided we'd just take a change of clothes and stay at the big house with y'all, just in case it snows real bad." She leaned toward the door to another room and called, "Jake, are you ready yet? Mr. Shaw done sent the young'uns for us. Hurry up, you hear?"

"I'm ready, be right there," Jake called from the other room. He came into the front room with a bag thrown across his shoulder and a lighted lantern.

Mrs. Burns picked up her bag from across the room and led the way out of the house. Jake went ahead with the light and Joe brought up the rear with his lantern. Mandie stayed back near Joe and let Polly get ahead of her.

"I hope nobody bothers my box, you know," Mandie whispered to Joe as they walked. "And I don't want other people to see it. Know what I mean?"

"You shouldn't have left it just sitting there at the back door," Joe told her under his breath.

"I know," she whispered. She would have to grab the box and hide it because she was afraid if Polly saw it and got the idea that it was a treasure map she would follow them around.

Also, she would have to talk to her grandmother about the Guyers. And she had not told Joe yet that Jonathan was coming to visit.

"Oh me, oh my!" she said under her breath to herself as the group moved on.

Chapter 6 / Up Went the Tree

Jake Burns led the way to the back of the Shaw house with his lantern to illuminate their path. Just as he started to open the door, Mandie stopped and said to Joe, "Let's go in the front door."

"But why?" Joe asked as he looked at her in the light from his lantern.

"Oh, you know, let's just go in the front door. It's nearer to the parlor," Mandie insisted. She started to walk around the house. "Come on, Polly."

"Well, all right, then," Joe agreed. "We'll catch up with y'all inside," he called back to the Burnses, who were going through the back way.

"If y'all are going in the front, then I will, too," Polly said. She quickly followed Joe and Mandie.

Mandie pushed open the front door, quickly removed her coat, hat, and gloves, and hung them on the hall tree. Joe and Polly did likewise.

As soon as they got to the parlor door, Mandie turned to look at Joe where Polly couldn't see her face and said, "I'll be right back." She mouthed the words "the box" and hurried down the hallway.

Polly followed Joe into the parlor.

Mandie went straight to the box she had left on the table at the back door. She looked around as she picked it up, trying to figure out where to hide it.

"The closet under the stairs," she murmured to herself as she quickly opened the door to the space under the steps leading up to the second floor. As she did, she was amazed at the contents of the place. There was not one inch of space to store the box. Linens were packed tightly into every shelf, and the space on the floor beneath was covered with canned goods stacked all the way up to the bottom shelf. "How did anyone ever figure out how to put all this into one closet?" she said aloud.

Closing the closet door, she glanced around the hallway. Then she realized the table had a large drawer. She pulled it open and breathed a sigh of relief when she found it empty, but the box just barely fit inside.

"Mandie, your mother is asking where you are," Polly called to her as she came down the corridor.

"I'm coming," Mandie said, trying to close the drawer.

"What are you doing?" Polly asked as she came closer.

"Nothing," Mandie said, moving in front of the drawer. "This drawer is stuck. Why don't you go back and tell my mother I'll be right there?"

Polly had come up to her and bent forward to see into the drawer. "What's wrong with the drawer, Mandie?"

"Oh, Polly, please go back to the parlor," Mandie said as she let go of the drawer and turned to stand in front of it.

Polly managed to see behind Mandie. "No wonder it won't close," she said. "What is that inside? It's too big for the drawer."

Mandie gave up, turned around, and took the box out of the drawer. "It's just a box I was trying to put away," she said, holding it with both hands. "Come on. I'm going back to the parlor."

Mandie hastened down the hallway and Polly followed.

"What's in the box, Mandie?" Polly asked as she looked at Mandie.

"Nothing important," Mandie replied and kept right on into the parlor. She looked around for a place to put the box. Everyone was there, and everyone was involved in some chore of decorating. The tree had been placed in the pot and was standing at the other side of the room away from the heat of the fireplace. Joe and Abraham were bringing in buckets of dirt and pouring it into the pot as Uncle John held the tree in place. Dr. Woodard was on a ladder while Elizabeth and Mrs. Taft handed him pieces of greenery to place over the top of the window. Aunt Lou, Jenny, and Liza were untangling bundles of holly and mistletoe. Jake and Ludie Burns were darting among everyone for odds and ends as needed. Uncle Ned was stringing beads for the tree. Mrs. Woodard was standing back and giving directions for placement of everything.

Elizabeth looked across the room and asked, "Amanda, aren't you going to participate? And Polly?"

"Of course, Mother," Mandie said. She put the box on a table and sat down on the carpet to assist in separating the holly and mistletoe.

"Yes, ma'am," Polly said as she went to help pass the greenery to Dr. Woodard.

Mandie stayed within view of her box and watched Polly moving about the room. And when they finally got to the task of decorating the tree, Elizabeth surveyed their work around the room and said, "I believe we could take a break now for refreshments."

"Hot cocoa," Joe spoke up as he stood by Mandie near the table with the box on it.

"With marshmallows," Mandie added.

"Suppose we get some sticks and roast the marshmallows over the fire? What do y'all think?" Uncle John asked as he looked around the room.

"Yes!" Mandie agreed with a big smile.

"I'll get the sticks," Joe volunteered as he started toward the door.

"I believe you'll find plenty of sticks in the leftovers on the back porch," John Shaw told him.

"I'll help make the hot cocoa," Mrs. Taft said, and as she glanced at her hands, she added, "As soon as I wash my dirty hands."

Mandie looked at her grandmother in surprise. She had never seen the woman do any kind of work. She had servants at her home. Her many businesses kept her involved and she had never seemed interested in housework.

"If you are going to make the hot cocoa, then I'd better go along to supervise," Mandie teased with a big grin.

Mrs. Taft didn't blink an eye as she replied, also grinning, "That might be a good idea. Let's go." She started toward the door.

Aunt Lou had stood by listening to the conversation, and she said, "Now, I don't be needin' no-body else in my kitchen. I'll make dat hot cocoa myself. Come along, Liza." She started for the door and beckoned to Liza.

"Then we'll just go and watch," Mrs. Taft told her.

Without remembering about the box, Mandie followed them to the kitchen. She helped Liza get down cups and saucers, and Mrs. Taft stood by watching.

"One of these days I need to take time to learn a few things about food and the operation of a kitchen," Mrs. Taft remarked as Aunt Lou added more water to the kettle and set it on a hot cap.

"Ain't nuthin' to it, really," Aunt Lou told her. "But if I may say, ma'am, a lady in yo' position don't need to be wastin' huh time in de kitchen. People like us needs our jobs in de kitchen, and people like you gotta make de money to keep de kitchen goin'."

"Dat's right. Cain't nobody do ev'ything," Liza joined in from across the room.

"I'll teach you if you really want to learn, Grand-mother," Mandie said. "Aunt Lou taught me, you know, and I wrote up all the recipes. We put them together and got it made into a book that we call *Mandie's Cookbook*."*

"Why, Amanda, that would be wonderful," Mrs. Taft told her. "When you grow up you will have a well-rounded education."

Liza took large bags of marshmallows from the cabinet and asked Mandie, "What you wantin' to do wid dese?"

---

*For more information on *Mandie's Cookbook* see page 175.

Mandie rushed to take them from her and said, "I need a large platter to put these on and some little tea plates for everyone to hold them after we roast them." She helped Liza find the proper dishes.

Liza looked at Aunt Lou and Mrs. Taft and then leaned over to whisper to Mandie, "You dun left dat Miss Sweet Thing in de parlor wid de doctuh's son."

Mandie gasped as she thought about the box she had left on the table. "I'd better go back and help Joe with the sticks," she said as she hurried out of the kitchen.

She met up with Joe and Polly in the hallway on their way back to the parlor with sticks for roasting the marshmallows.

"Aunt Lou is making the hot cocoa," Mandie remarked as she joined them.

"I didn't think she would need you to help," Joe teased.

"No, not really," Mandie replied when they came to the door of the parlor. She rushed into the room and went to look at her box. It was still on the table and didn't look as though it had been disturbed.

"I didn't touch your old box," Polly said as she watched Mandie.

"Why, Polly, I didn't say you did," Mandie told her.

Uncle John and Uncle Ned came into the room then carrying boxes full of decorations, which they set down near the tree.

"Did you all get those from the attic?" Mandie asked.

"We sure did," John Shaw told her, dusting off his hands.

"I saw them up there one time. Lots of the stuff

must be awfully old," Mandie replied as she bent to look into one of the boxes.

"As old as this house," John Shaw said.

"And some older than grandfather of John Shaw," Uncle Ned said.

"That would be terribly old," Dr. Woodard added from the doorway where he had come in. "And I suppose you young people will want to know the story of each piece." He looked at Mandie, Joe, and Polly.

"I'm afraid that would take all night," John Shaw said with a laugh. "We can't possibly use all this, so Amanda, Joe, and Polly can just pick out what they want to hang on the tree."

Aunt Lou and Liza brought trays holding the hot cocoa and marshmallows and set them on a long table. Mrs. Taft followed with the white linen napkins, which she placed alongside the trays.

Mandie watched her grandmother and with a smile said, "Well, Grandmother, you did get to help after all."

Mrs. Taft responded with a big smile of her own.

At that moment Jason Bond entered the parlor. "Hope you don't mind I took so long," he said to John Shaw as he came to stand by the fireplace. "There are so many wonderful people over that mountain, and I just had to visit awhile."

"Oh no, that's quite all right," John Shaw replied. "You're back just in time for a hot drink and to help decorate the tree."

"It's cold outside and still looks like snow," Jason Bond told him. "Now, what can I do around here?"

Mandie spoke up. "Help us tie the ribbons on the decorations," she said. "Look at all those things in these boxes. We have to go through it all and pick out whatever the tree will hold." She pointed to the boxes nearby.

"Looks like a big job," Jason Bond said with a smile as he bent to inspect the contents.

"Shall we get started now? Otherwise we're going to be all night getting this tree decorated," Elizabeth Shaw said loudly as she looked around the room. "Help yourselves to the cocoa and cookies. We can stop now and then to roast a marshmallow in the fireplace whenever you wish."

Everyone immediately pitched in and the hot cocoa and cookies soon disappeared. Aunt Lou and Liza went back to the kitchen for more.

Mandie excitedly picked out items in the boxes and tied red ribbons around them with a loop to put over a branch of the tree, but she kept watching her box on the table.

When the decorating job came to an end, everyone stood back to admire their work. Elizabeth went to the piano and began playing Christmas carols. Soon the whole crowd was taking part in the singing.

As the grandfather clock in the hallway struck midnight, Elizabeth stood up and said, "This has been a wonderful day, but I think we'd better all retire now. Otherwise, we may fall asleep at church tomorrow." She laughed as she looked around the room, and the others joined in.

Uncle John looked at Polly and said, "Now, Miss Polly, we'll send someone to escort you home. It's late." He looked directly at Joe.

Mandie quickly offered, "I will go with her, Uncle John."

"Then who is going to escort you back home?"

her uncle teased. "I think we'd better let someone else go."

Mandie walked over to Uncle Ned, looked up at him with her blue eyes, and asked, "Uncle Ned, would you mind walking with me and Polly over to her house?"

"I be glad to go," the old man told her.

As they put on their coats and hats in the hall-way, Polly called back to Joe, "Aren't you coming with us, Joe?"

Joe walked over to the doorway and said with a big grin, "I wasn't exactly asked. See you later." He stepped back into the parlor.

"Well, he could have come anyway," Polly muttered as she followed Mandie and Uncle Ned out the front door.

Outside the moon could barely be seen behind the clouds floating over it. And as Jason Bond had said, it was terribly cold.

Mandie held Uncle Ned's hand as they walked through the trees to Polly's house. Although Polly lived next door, it was still a good distance from the Shaws' house.

"I have my presents all wrapped for you to take to my Cherokee kinpeople, Uncle Ned. I put them in flour sacks in my room," she told him.

Before he could say anything, Polly said quickly, "I don't understand why you put red paper on all of them—every single one. Why didn't you use differ-ent colors like green or white?"

Mandie gasped with surprise. "And how do you know what I wrapped my presents with?" she asked, looking at the girl on the other side of Uncle Ned.

"Well, I . . . I do, anyhow, I—" Polly stuttered.

"So you *had* been in my room when I saw you in the hallway," Mandie said. "Why did you go snooping in my room?"

"But, Mandie, I was only looking for you," Polly said quickly. "You were gone so long I figured you weren't coming back right away."

"I was not gone all that long," Mandie argued.

"Let us not say angry words," Uncle Ned said as he squeezed Mandie's hand and reached to clasp Polly's with his other. "Must remember. Think first."

Mandie breathed deeply and said, "I'm sorry, Polly. I suppose I'm just tired, and there are some things bothering me that you don't know about."

"That's all right, Mandie," Polly replied. "You know I always like to be part of whatever is going on."

"I go home when sun rises," Uncle Ned said. "Must promise no angry words while I go to bring back Sallie and Morning Star."

Mandie wondered how she would ever be able to hold down her temper when Polly was always doing irritating things. Maybe if she could just ignore Polly altogether, she would be able to overlook what Polly said and did.

"I promise to try, Uncle Ned," Mandie told the old Indian as they continued through the adjoining yards. "I'm really anxious to see Sallie, and Morning Star, too, of course. And I'm so glad you all will be here to celebrate Christmas with us."

Uncle Ned looked down at Polly, who had been silent. Polly caught his glance and said, "I always try to behave."

They came to the front door of Polly's house, and her mother answered their knock. She insisted they come in, but Mandie quickly declined.

"We have to get back. It's too late, but thank you, Mrs. Cornwallis. We'll be over tomorrow night to help decorate your tree," Mandie told her.

"Please don't let your mother forget," Mrs. Cornwallis said, and looking up at Uncle Ned, she said, "Thank you for walking Polly home."

"Welcome," the old man said.

As Mandie and Uncle Ned started to turn and walk off the porch, Polly called to Mandie from the doorway, "I don't know why you are so protective of that old box. It's just full of dirt and twigs. What good could it be?"

Mandie instantly stopped, turned around, and was about to give an angry reply when Polly shut the door.

"So she has managed to look in my box," Mandie said as she followed Uncle Ned off the porch.

"No damage done," Uncle Ned said, leading the way down the pathway. "No one know what is in box anyhow. Look like what she said."

"Oh, but, Uncle Ned, Joe and I have been trying to figure out whether it's a treasure map or not, and I didn't want Polly to know because she follows us around every minute when Joe is here," Mandie told him.

"But she might help figure out," the old man said.

"Oh well," Mandie said, giving up the subject.

Uncle Ned paused as they came to the front steps of the Shaw house. "What things bothering Papoose? Must settle bothering things," he said.

Mandie stopped by his side, then sat down on a step, and he joined her. "I have big problems, Uncle Ned," Mandie began. "You see, when I was in New York I asked Mr. Guyer and Jonathan to come visit with us for Christmas, and my mother said she received a note saying they were coming." She paused.

"That no problem," Uncle Ned said.

"But it's all so complicated," Mandie tried to explain. "You see, for some reason my grandmother does not like Mr. Guyer. I don't know what will happen when he and Jonathan arrive and my grandmother has to stay under the same roof with them for a few days."

"Still no problem," Uncle Ned insisted. "So many company they do not have to talk."

"And then there's Joe," Mandie added. "I don't know if you noticed when Joe and Jonathan met in New York, but they didn't seem to like each other, and they will both be here during Christmas. Like you have always told me, I should have thought first before I asked the Guyers to come visit."

"Still no problem, Papoose," the old man said. "They will all get to be friends before they leave John Shaw's house."

"Oh, and, Uncle Ned, Grandmother doesn't know they are coming, and neither does Joe. I haven't told them yet," Mandie said with a big sigh.

"Papoose should tell right away so no surprise," Uncle Ned replied.

"I haven't had a chance to talk to Grandmother since I left school to come home. She's always busy. And I've been wondering how to tell Joe," Mandie said.

"Must tell all," the old man said. "First sunup go tell. Must not let Guyers be surprise."

"I know," Mandie agreed. "I'll have to figure out how to get Grandmother to stand still long enough to explain to her. But what if she decides to pack up and leave because the Guyers are coming?"

"Grandmother of Papoose will not pack up and leave. She come to celebrate with daughter and granddaughter. She will not go home," Uncle Ned said.

"I don't think the Woodards would leave because the Guyers are coming, because Dr. Woodard and Jonathan's father seemed to get along fine in New York when they met," Mandie said. "But you know how jealous Joe is. He wants to marry me when we grow up."

Uncle Ned smiled as he looked at her. "Long time away," he said. "Many other boys go through life of Papoose before grown up. He knows that."

"Yes, and when he goes away to the university, I suppose he will meet lots of other girls, too," Mandie said thoughtfully. She secretly felt a pain of jealousy as she thought about that.

Uncle Ned stood up, and Mandie joined him. He looked around the yard and asked, "Where white cat? Not see all time we decorate."

"Snowball!" Mandie said as she suddenly realized he had not been around that night. "I hope he's on my bed. No, that couldn't be because I closed my door after he got in my room and tore up all the paper on my gifts. I'll have to go find him." She quickly went up the steps and through the front door.

"Good night, Uncle Ned," Mandie replied as she went toward the kitchen. "I'll be up in the morning to tell you good-bye."

Mandie opened the kitchen door and was relieved to find her white cat curled up on top of the box of wood by the warmth of the big iron cookstove where a fire was kept twenty-four hours a day during cold weather.

"Snowball, it's time to go to bed," Mandie said, stooping down to pick him up. He opened his eyes, looked at her, and tried to go back to sleep.

As she hurried toward her room, she thought about what Uncle Ned had said. She had to get the dreaded task over with. She had to tell her grandmother and Joe that the Guyers were coming without further delay.

Chapter 7 / A Misunderstanding

The next morning everyone was up earlier than usual because Uncle Ned wanted to leave by daybreak. Mandie jumped out of bed as soon as Liza came into her room to build up the fire in the fireplace. Snowball stretched, yawned, and followed his mistress as she sat on the carpet in the warmth from the fire.

"Good morning, Liza," she greeted the young maid. "Have you been in my grandmother's room yet? Is she up?"

"Mawnin', Missy 'Manda," Liza said, adding a log to the fire. "Now, dat lady she dun went and got dressed and dun went down to de parlor soon as I shake up huh fire."

"Oh shucks!" Mandie exclaimed as she jumped to her feet. "I was hoping to catch her before she left her room." She went to the wardrobe to take down a dress.

"Well, now, you kin ketch huh in de parlor," Liza

said. "I gotta go now." She walked over to the door.

"Thanks, Liza," Mandie said as she quickly dressed. "I'll see you downstairs."

Liza left the room, and Mandie hurriedly brushed her long blond hair and tied it back with a red ribbon to match her red calico dress. She glanced in the mirror one last time as she shook out the folds in her long, gathered skirt.

"Come on, Snowball," she said as she opened the door. "We're going to eat, and I've got to talk to Grandmother first if I can get her alone."

Snowball quickly darted past her feet into the hallway and was out of sight by the time she closed the door.

Mandie hurried downstairs to the parlor and was disappointed to find not only her grandmother there but all three Woodards, Uncle John, and Uncle Ned.

"Good morning," she greeted everyone as she entered the room and went to sit near Joe as everyone returned her greeting.

"Sleepyhead!" Joe teased.

"I'm up earlier than usual. Everybody else must have stayed up all night," Mandie told him. She glanced at Uncle Ned with a frown and disappointed look as he made a slight nod in the direction of her grandmother.

"I didn't. I was the last one down before you," Joe replied.

Mandie looked over at the adults who were clustered around the fireplace. They were busy with their own conversation. She could talk to Joe right now about the Guyers without her grandmother overhearing her. And she certainly needed to get her grandmother alone because there was no telling what kind of response she would get from her.

"Joe, there's something I need to say to you," Mandie began in a low voice.

Joe immediately looked at her, smiled, and said, "I'm listening."

At that moment there was a loud knock on the front door and everyone stopped talking when they heard it. Then Mandie could hear Liza opening the front door and saying, "Good mawnin'. Whut kin I be doin' fo' you?"

There was a loud laugh, and Mandie heard Jonathan Guyer say, "You must be Liza."

"And you must be dat Yankee boy and man we be expectin'," Liza replied with a slight giggle. "Y'all come right in now, you heah?"

Mandie's heart did flip-flops and she felt short of breath. She looked at her grandmother, who was saying, "I do believe you have company, John."

"Yes," John Shaw said as he rose and went to the parlor door to greet Mr. Guyer and Jonathan, who were waiting there. "Welcome! I'm John Shaw, Amanda's uncle, and I do believe you're Lindall Guyer and Jonathan. We've heard so much about you. Please give Liza your coats and come on in and join us."

"Glad to meet you," Lindall Guyer said as he removed his coat and handed it to Liza.

"So am I, sir," Jonathan said as he hung his coat and hat on the hall tree.

As the Guyers came into the parlor, Jonathan immediately spotted Mandie and came to sit by her and Joe.

"I'm glad you could come, Jonathan. You remember Joe, don't you?" Mandie said, nervously watching both of the boys. "Joe, you were at Jonathan's house in New York, remember?"

"Sure I remember Joe," Jonathan said, extending his hand. "How are you?"

"Fine. And how are you?" Joe asked as he shook hands with him.

Mandie glanced over at the adults and heard her grandmother say, "Why, Lindall Guyer, I had no idea you would be coming here." She had a slight smile on her face.

"First time I've been to visit the Shaws here," Lindall said as he sat down by John Shaw. He turned to greet Uncle Ned and Dr. Woodard. "Glad to see you again."

Dr. Woodard introduced his wife, and Mandie caught a glimpse of Liza peeking around the door. The girl had always been curious about the Guyers since Mandie had come back from Europe the summer before and told Liza about becoming acquainted with Jonathan and his father.

"Y'all are just in time for breakfast," Mandie told Jonathan, trying to ease the tension between the two boys.

"Hope you have lots to eat. I'm hungry," Jonathan said with a laugh.

"So am I," Joe finally spoke.

Mandie looked back at the doorway and saw her mother coming into the room. As John Shaw stood up, Lindall Guyer also rose and looked at Elizabeth, who was coming toward him with her hand extended.

"We're delighted that you and Jonathan could come," Elizabeth said. Then she glanced at Jonathan and smiled.

"This is my wife, Elizabeth," John Shaw told Mr. Guyer.

"How do you do?" Lindall said, shaking her hand.

Turning to John, Elizabeth said, "I've met Mr. Guyer before, a long time ago."

"We've met before?" Lindall questioned her.

"Yes, years ago when you came to my mother's house. That's my mother over there, Mrs. Norman Taft," Elizabeth explained.

"Oh, goodness gracious, yes!" Lindall exclaimed. "How dumb of me not to realize who you were. I knew Amanda was Mrs. Taft's granddaughter, but I didn't realize who her mother was. I apologize."

"That's quite all right. It has been a long time," Elizabeth said. "Why don't we sit down and get comfortable until breakfast is ready?" She sat down nearby, and Lindall sat across from her.

"I'll see to your luggage," John Shaw offered as he remained standing.

"I hired a rig, and the driver dropped it inside your front hallway," Lindall Guyer said, standing up. "I'll go with you."

As the two men left the parlor, Mandie glanced at her grandmother, who was silently staring into the flames in the fireplace. *So Lindall Guyer had been to Grandmother's house years ago*, she thought. *They must have been friends back then. What happened to make Grandmother dislike him?* She sure would like to know.

"Have you decided about a college? Are you coming to New York to attend one?" Jonathan asked Joe.

"No, that place is too big for me," Joe replied. "We're still looking, but not in New York."

Mandie noticed how the two boys were looking

each other over. She knew she was going to be miserable with both of them around. Glancing at her grandmother again, Mandie saw that she was not taking part in the conversation among the other adults.

Feeling the tension rising between the two boys, Mandie suddenly remembered her box. She jumped up, went over to the table where she had put it, and brought it back to show to Jonathan.

"Look at this," she told him as she removed the lid. "Someone wrapped this stuff up like a gift and left it on the doorstep with my name on it yesterday." She held the box out to him.

Jonathan looked but didn't take the box. He shrugged his shoulders and asked, "Well, what is it supposed to be?"

"I don't know, but Joe and I decided it must be a treasure map of some kind," she replied.

"You mean *you* decided that. I was only teasing when I said it must be a treasure map," Joe reminded her.

"Well, anyhow, we've been outside with it, trying to figure out if these tiny little trenches in the dirt could represent roads," Mandie said, indicating the places in the box. "And these ribbons must be landmarks or something to mark the way to whatever or wherever the treasure is." She looked at him.

Jonathan was grinning as he replied, "You figure it all out, not me."

"Oh, you're acting just like Joe. He doesn't want to help, either," Mandie said with a big sigh as she looked at Joe.

Joe laughed and said, "I didn't say I wouldn't help. I said I'd go along with you while you solve the mystery."

"When are you beginning this search, or whatever you wish to call it?" Jonathan asked.

"This afternoon," Mandie said. "That is, if it doesn't snow. We have to go to church this morning, and then after we come home and eat, we can begin. Are you coming with us?"

"Well, you know, I'm not very good at such stuff," Jonathan said with a big grin.

At that moment Aunt Lou came to the doorway to announce, "Miz 'Lizbeth, breakfust is served."

Elizabeth rose and replied, "Aunt Lou, thank you. Could you please find Mr. Shaw and Mr. Guyer and tell them for me?" She sat back down.

"Yes, ma'am," Aunt Lou answered and went on down the hallway.

"So that was Aunt Lou?" Jonathan said.

"Yes, that was Aunt Lou. Sooner or later you'll meet all the people who live here," Mandie told him.

"I've heard so much about them I feel like I know them already," Jonathan said.

"But we don't have nearly as many people working here as you and your father do," Mandie said. "And all our people speak southern English, no foreigners in this house." She laughed.

"And no southerners in our house," Jonathan replied.

"Just what little time I was there I couldn't understand half of what those people in New York were saying," Joe remarked. "They talk too fast and with their hands."

"How is Angelina?" Mandie asked. She was a runaway girl in New York who had claimed a dog that had wandered into Jonathan's backyard during Mandie's visit at Thanksgiving time.

"Oh, she's fine," Jonathan replied. "But she still

wants to claim Whitey, and I have to keep telling her the dog's owner gave him to me."

At that moment John Shaw and Lindall Guyer came back into the parlor.

"I heard the food is on the table," John said to Elizabeth, who immediately rose from her chair.

"Yes, let's go in before everything gets cold, shall we?" Elizabeth said, looking about the room at her guests.

After they were all seated at the table and conversation began again, Mandie noticed that her grandmother was still not participating. Evidently she was awfully upset with the presence of the Guyers. Mandie dreaded the thought of the lady catching her alone and venting that anger on her.

After the meal was over, Uncle Ned left for his home, promising to return. Everyone went to their rooms to dress for church services. Mandie hurried through changing her clothes, planning to come back down to the parlor to meet Jonathan and Joe. She hoped her grandmother would not stop her on the way.

She was brushing her hair when someone tapped on her door. Her heartbeat quickened as she called, "Come in."

The door slowly opened, and Liza slipped inside the room, closing it behind her. She put her finger to her lips, signaling to be quiet.

"What's wrong?" Mandie asked in a soft voice.

"I ain't s'pose to be heah," the girl told her. "But I jes' had dis heah idea after I dun seen dat Noo Yawk boy." She came closer to Mandie.

"Liza, what are you up to?" Mandie asked with a laugh.

"I ain't up to nuthin, Missy 'Manda," Liza replied

as she placed her hands on her thin hips. "But like I was sayin', I knows whut we kin do 'bout dat Miss Sweet Thing."

"I have to hurry, Liza, and get back down to the parlor," Mandie said as she pinned her hair up. She would be wearing a hat to church.

"Well, dis won't take but a minute if you'd jes' listen," the girl insisted as she followed Mandie to the wardrobe, where Mandie took down her best coat.

"Then tell me what you're talking about, Liza," Mandie said. "I have to get back downstairs, and come to think of it, you'd better be getting ready yourself for church."

"Dat won't take but a minute," Liza said. "You see, I been thinkin' 'bout dat Noo Yawk boy. I think dat Miss Sweet Thing might roll her eyes at him. He ain't bad lookin'. What do you be thinkin' 'bout dat?"

Mandie smiled as she looked at Liza. "You sure come up with some ideas," she said as she took her hat out of the hatbox in the bottom of her wardrobe. "So you believe Polly might be interested in Jonathan. Now, tell me how that matters to me. If she wants to be friends with Jonathan, that's all right with me." She stepped in front of the mirror to put on her hat and secured it with a large hatpin.

"Don't you even unnerstand whut I be tellin' you?" Liza asked. "Dat Miss Sweet Thing git to rollin' dem black eyes at dat Noo Yawk boy, den she leave doctuh's son alone." She grinned at Mandie and danced around the room.

"Liza, I can't make Polly like Jonathan," Mandie insisted. "She will probably be hanging around during the holidays anyway because Joe is here and I'm home from school."

"Den maybe dat Noo Yawk boy will like huh," Liza said. "And maybe dey won't follow you and doctuh's son around."

"We'll see," Mandie replied, trying to end the conversation. She picked up her coat and gloves and headed for the door. "Liza, you had better go get dressed for church or Aunt Lou is going to be awfully put out with you."

"I see you aftuh church," Liza promised as she darted out the door and down the hallway ahead of Mandie.

Mandie smiled to herself as she went down to the parlor. Liza seemed more interested in matching up boys and girls than she was in finding a boy for herself. And as far as Mandie knew, Liza had never had a boyfriend. She was older than Mandie and was old enough to be interested in boys. But Mandie knew Liza had been orphaned when she was small, then Aunt Lou had taken her under her wing, and Aunt Lou could be awfully strict sometimes.

When Mandie got to the parlor, she found Uncle John and Dr. Woodard already there. She was about to sit down when Joe and Jonathan came in together. She noticed they were walking along together but didn't seem to be engaged in any conversation. She wished they would get to be friends because they were both her friends.

"My, my! You absolutely look beautiful! What did you do to yourself?" Jonathan teased as he and Joe sat down near her.

"I only put on my Sunday clothes, Jonathan Guyer," Mandie replied with a big smile. "What have you done to yourself? You look different some-how.''

"Oh, I am different,'' Jonathan answered, grin-ning. "I changed clothes, too, and even combed my hair.'' He patted the dark curls on top of his head.

Joe had been listening and watching but had not said a word. Now he spoke. "I've been outside,'' he said. "It still looks like snow.''

"I hope it doesn't snow before Uncle Ned comes back with Morning Star and Sallie,'' Mandie re-marked. "They might have a rough journey across that mountain.''

"But then after they get here, I hope it snows for Christmas,'' Joe said.

"It snows so much in New York that it usually doesn't miss a Christmas,'' Jonathan said.

"But if it snows, we won't be able to get out and see if we can figure out that treasure map,'' Mandie reminded them.

"I wish I knew who sent you that mess,'' Joe re-marked.

"Why?'' Mandie asked.

"Because I'd make them explain what it's all about,'' Joe replied.

"Well, don't you like treasure maps? The way Mandie tells me things, I thought you both liked treasure maps,'' Jonathan said.

"But we don't know that that thing in the box is a real treasure map,'' Joe said.

"We'll just have to study it and work on it to see what it is exactly,'' Mandie said.

"I would say I'd help you, but I don't know any-thing about treasure maps,'' Jonathan told her. "I've never had one.''

"Be thankful you haven't,'' Joe said. "These

things cause a lot of hard work and trouble, and they're not always worth it.''

"Oh, they're a lot of fun anyway, even if you don't find much of anything at the end of the trail," Mandie said. "We'll work on it this afternoon if it doesn't snow."

Mandie secretly wondered if that thing really was a treasure map, but she wouldn't admit that to anyone. It would give them something interesting to do together.

Elizabeth, Mrs. Woodard, and Mrs. Taft came into the parlor then, and John Shaw rose to say, "We are all ready and waiting. I believe it's about time to go."

When they got to the church, Mandie noticed that her grandmother stepped into the pew first with Elizabeth right behind her. Evidently she wanted to be sure she didn't sit next to Lindall Guyer. Mandie found herself between Joe and Jonathan when they all sat down.

The pastor's sermon was about forgiveness, and his voice was loud and clear. Mandie knew her grandmother couldn't help hearing him, although Mrs. Taft's attention seemed to stray to the other side of the church away from the direction of Lindall Guyer. And when they stood to sing hymns, Mrs. Taft sang as she usually did, although she kept her eyes focused on the book.

When the service was over and they returned to the house, Mrs. Taft went straight to her room with the remark that she would be right back.

Mandie knew the servants were not required to cook on Sunday. The meal had been prepared on Saturday, as it always was, and then warmed up on Sunday. Everyone pitched in to help. The servants' church held services longer than their church, so the Shaw family was usually finished when the others came home. Elizabeth was trying to hurry things up, and Mrs. Woodard helped.

Mandie volunteered to do whatever was needed to be done, and she was surprised when Jonathan and Joe both asked to help. Elizabeth had them carry food to the table.

"So many volunteers today," Elizabeth said with a smile. "Amanda, if you would just go hurry up your grandmother a little bit, we're about ready to eat."

Mandie's heart sank. "Go get Grandmother?" she asked.

"Yes, just tell her it's all ready," Elizabeth said. "And hurry back, dear."

"Yes, ma'am," Mandie reluctantly agreed as she headed toward the door.

She hurried up the steps and down the hallway to the door of her grandmother's room. Knocking first, she called through the door, "Mother says everything is ready."

Mrs. Taft opened the door and stood there looking at Mandie with a frown.

"It's all ready, Grandmother," Mandie said, starting to turn and leave.

"Wait," Mrs. Taft said quickly.

"Yes, Grandmother?" Mandie said, turning back to look at her.

"I'm coming," Mrs. Taft said, closing the door to her room as she stepped into the hallway. "I'm just wondering why your mother didn't tell me she had invited Lindall Guyer to spend Christmas with us?"

"Mother?" Mandie questioned as they walked down the corridor.

"She should have warned me," Mrs. Taft continued.

"I'm sorry, Grandmother," Mandie said, suddenly deciding not to tell her grandmother that she had invited the Guyers.

Mandie knew her grandmother wouldn't dare confront her daughter over anything in her daughter's house. So just maybe, as long as Mrs. Taft thought Elizabeth had invited the Guyers, Mandie wouldn't have to worry about it any longer. Yes, she decided, that would be the best solution for now.

Chapter 8 / Is It a Map or Not?

When the meal was finished, the adults went to the parlor, and Mandie asked Jonathan and Joe to go outside with her to begin the treasure hunt. She carefully carried the box, and the three young people looked at the mess inside it now and then as they walked along the road.

When they came to the crossroads where she and Joe had been the day before, Mandie stopped and asked the boys, "Which way do y'all think we ought to go?" She held the box out for them to look inside.

The two boys looked at it and then at each other. They answered at the same time.

"That way," Jonathan said, pointing to the left.

"That way," Joe said, pointing to the right.

"Oh, what am I supposed to do? Y'all don't agree," Mandie said.

"You choose which way," Jonathan told her.

"Yes, Mandie, you decide," Joe said.

107

"No, I can't do that," Mandie said in exasperation. "If I decide to go to the left, then you, Joe, will be put out with me because that's the direction Jonathan picked. And you, Jonathan, won't like it if I choose Joe's way."

At that moment Snowball came running up to join them and began rubbing around Mandie's ankles.

"No, it's all right with me whichever way you want to go," Jonathan insisted.

"And you know that I'm just going along and leaving it up to you to decide which way we're going about this," Joe reminded her.

Snowball stood up on his hind paws and held on to the hem of Mandie's skirt. He started meowing loudly.

"Oh, Snowball, get down and hush up," Mandie told him as she stepped away from him.

The white cat growled angrily for a moment and then turned and raced off down the road to the right.

"Snowball, come back here," Mandie called after him.

"Come on. He just made the decision about which road to take. Let's follow him," Joe said with a laugh.

The three hurried after the white cat. Snowball paused to look back at them, and when they almost caught up, he raced off again and turned to look back.

Finally, Mandie stopped in the middle of the road, took a deep breath, and said, "He thinks we're playing a game with him. Let's just ignore him, but I'll keep an eye on him." She looked down at the contents of the box she was carrying. "Let's see if we can figure out where we are on this map."

"Well, now, if you're claiming those little indentations are roads, then we must be here," Joe said, pointing to a bunch of twigs in the dirt inside the box.

Jonathan was silent.

Mandie asked, "Well, Jonathan?"

"Oh, I agree with Joe. I don't know how to read a treasure map," Jonathan said with a big grin. "You will have to figure it out."

"You could at least guess," Mandie said with a little smile.

"But I did guess. I made the same guess that Joe did," Jonathan insisted.

"All right, then," Mandie said, looking back down at the inside of the box. "If we're right there, then I suppose we should go down that road to the left that is coming up down yonder." She looked ahead. She also noticed Snowball had stopped running and was sitting in the road watching them.

"Agreed," Joe said.

"Yes," Jonathan added.

Mandie suddenly heard her name being called behind them. She turned to look back and saw Liza running down the road toward her.

"Missy 'Manda!" Liza was calling as she held up her long skirt and ran toward the three young people. When she came up to Mandie, she had to pause to get her breath.

"What's wrong, Liza?" Mandie asked anxiously.

"Ain't nuthin' wrong. It's jes' dat I has to ax you sumthin'," Liza said, looking at the two boys.

"Well, what is it?" Mandie asked.

Liza stepped between Mandie and the boys and whispered, "I has to tell you private like. Over heah." She moved over to the side of the road.

Mandie followed as she frowned and asked again, "What is it, Liza?"

"Well, you see, dat Miss Sweet Thing, she be at de house lookin' fo' you, and I tells huh you be out walkin' round," Liza replied.

"Did she go back to her house?" Mandie asked.

"Nope," Liza replied. "I tell huh to wait, and I sees if I kin find you."

"Well, now you've found me, Liza," Mandie said. She glanced at Joe and Jonathan. They were looking at her from across the road.

"Well, whut I wants to know is, does you want dat Miss Sweet Thing to find you, being as how you got doctuh's son and dat Yankee boy both out for a walk?" Liza asked.

"Oh, Liza, you don't have to go to so much trouble for me," Mandie said. "It's all right if you tell her where I am. I don't want you to lie about it. I'm not really anxious for her to find out what we're doing, but I suppose sooner or later she'll know anyway."

"Whut you doin'?" Liza asked as she looked at the box in Mandie's hands.

"Liza, this is that present I received. We're trying to figure out whether it's a treasure map or not. In other words, we're trying to trace out these little lines in it and see where they go," Mandie explained.

"Oh, I 'member dat uttuh treasure map whut you had one time, and I he'ped you find dat treasure, 'member?" Liza said, smiling.

"I remember, and you could help us with this one, but I know Aunt Lou is too busy and you have to help her," Mandie said. "I'll let you know if it all works out as a real treasure map."

"Den I goes back and tells dat Miss Sweet Thing

you down heah," Liza said. She turned to go back up the road.

"Liza, please don't tell her we're looking for a treasure because I'm not sure this is even a real treasure map," Mandie called after her.

"I won't," Liza promised as she hurried back toward the house.

Mandie stepped over to join the two boys. Looking at Joe, she explained, "Polly is at the house asking for me, and Liza didn't know whether or not to tell her where I am, so I said go ahead and tell her. I suppose she will join us shortly." Then turning to Jonathan, she explained, "Polly Cornwallis is my next-door neighbor. I might have mentioned her sometime or other to you."

"I believe I've heard the name," Jonathan replied.

Mandie looked up the road as they stood there and saw Polly hurrying toward them. "Here she comes," Mandie said.

"Liza told me y'all were out walking," Polly said as she gazed at Jonathan. He stared back at her.

"Polly, this is Jonathan Guyer, our friend from New York," Mandie introduced them. "He and his father are visiting us for the Christmas holidays. Jonathan, Polly Cornwallis."

"I heard y'all had some company from New York. I'm glad to meet you, Jonathan," Polly said, still looking him over.

"I'm pleased to make your acquaintance," Jonathan said solemnly.

"Well, let's walk on," Mandie said.

They moved on down the road. Polly immediately fell in beside Joe, but she still looked at Jonathan now and then. Snowball waited for them.

When they got to the intersection of the road that they had discussed before Liza's arrival, Mandie asked, "Should we go down this road?" She glanced down at the box in her hands. They all stopped to look around.

Polly noticed then that Mandie was holding the box. "Mandie, why are you carrying that old box with the dirt in it?"

"Because I want to," Mandie replied without looking at her.

"But why?" Polly insisted. She tossed back her long, dark hair that was hanging below her tam and looked at the box with her black eyes.

"Because I want to, Polly," Mandie replied impatiently. "Don't you ever do anything just because you want to?"

"I suppose so," Polly reluctantly agreed. "But I wouldn't want to go around carrying a box full of dirt and all that mess. I would think it would be a silly idea for me to do that." She looked at Mandie on the other side of Joe.

"Oh, Polly!" Mandie exclaimed.

Jonathan looked at Polly and said, "I think it's a very good idea. Who knows? We might just find a pot of gold at the end."

Mandie took a deep breath as Jonathan said that because she knew she would have to explain now to Polly.

"A pot of gold?" Polly questioned him. "Don't tell me you think this thing is a treasure map with a pot of gold at the end. That's impossible!"

"Nothing's impossible," Jonathan replied as he glanced at Polly. "This thing, as you call it, could very well be a treasure map. And if it is, we won't know what treasure awaits us at the end unless we try to find it.''

"But that's just a pile of dirt and twigs in that box. It's not a real treasure map," Polly objected.

"Whoever said what form a treasure map could be in?" Jonathan asked her. "It could probably be traced in dirt, carved in wood, or written on paper, or whatever.''

"But Mandie doesn't even know who sent her this mess in the box," Polly told him. "It may be a trick.''

"If someone played a trick on Mandie with this thing here, I'd sure hate to be the one who did it," Joe said with a big laugh.

"Oh, Joe, I know you had nothing to do with this box. You weren't even here when it came," Mandie said. Then she turned to Jonathan and said, "And you weren't, either. But as for Polly, she was home when I received this so-called gift." She glanced from Joe to Jonathan and then to Polly.

"Well, thank you, ma'am," Joe teased.

"I'm glad you've figured that much out," Jonathan replied with a big grin.

Polly frowned as she gazed at Mandie and said, "Amanda Elizabeth Shaw, I have better things to do than fill up boxes with dirt.''

"I didn't say you had anything to do with this box," Mandie quickly replied. "I only said you were home when I received it.''

"Well, that's implying that I had something to do with it," Polly replied.

"Polly—" Mandie began.

Joe loudly interrupted, "Girls, are we going ahead with this, or are we going to stand here wasting time? Because if you're not going ahead I'm going back to the house.''

"And I will, too," Jonathan added.

"I'm sorry, everybody," Mandie said, looking around the group. She held the box out toward Polly. "Would you like to carry the box and help us trace the little ridges and ruts in the dirt?"

Polly backed off and said, "No, thank you. I might spill that dirt all over my coat. You carry it. I'll just follow along with y'all."

"Let's get on with it," Joe told the girls as he began walking down the intersecting road.

Mandie realized she was on edge with everyone. The tension of worrying over the reception the Guyers would receive from her grandmother and from Joe had her all wound up. So far Joe and Jonathan had been polite to each other, but she was hoping they would become friends. And her grandmother had more or less stayed to herself since the Guyers had arrived, believing it was her daughter, Elizabeth, who had invited the people in the first place. Mandie knew sooner or later she would have to explain to her grandmother that she had been the one who extended the invitation. And there was no telling what the lady's reaction would be.

"Mandie! Are you coming?" Joe called to her.

Mandie realized the other three had walked ahead, and now she hurried to catch up. Snowball followed.

The young people, led by Mandie, wandered on into the business section of Franklin, where all the shops were closed because it was Sunday. They looked through the windows of the stores and admired the trees and decorations on the streets.

Mandie completely forgot about the box she was carrying.

"I suppose we've done our treasure-map hunting for the day," Joe said, looking at Mandie as she stood before a shop that sold crafts made by local people.

"I can't see inside too well, but I imagine these people who own this shop will have Uncle Ned's people's baskets to sell. Mother said she and I would go buy some tomorrow," Mandie replied, trying to see through the glass window.

"I'd like to buy some of his baskets to take back to New York," Jonathan remarked.

"I'd like to come with you and your mother so I can buy some, too," Polly quickly told Mandie.

Suddenly snow began falling. Large white flakes were rapidly covering everything. Mandie looked at her box and said, "Oh goodness, I need to put the lid on so this won't get all wet."

"Here, I'll help you," Joe said. "You hold the box, and I'll pull the lid out from under it."

"So I suppose that's the end of this so-called treasure hunt," Polly said as she tried to shake the snowflakes off her coat.

"I think it's the end of our walk today," Mandie said. "Mother said we should come back if it started to snow." She looked down at Snowball, who was rapidly blinking his blue eyes as the snowflakes fell into them. Handing the box to Joe, she said, "Here, if you'll carry the box, I'll carry Snowball so he won't get so wet from the snow." She picked the cat up and held him against her.

The four started back, and when they arrived at the Shaw gate, Mandie said, "Polly, we're coming to your house tonight to help decorate your tree, remember?"

"But I'm not going home right now," Polly quickly told her as she opened the gate and started up the long walkway. "Our company is old people, and I don't have anyone to talk to at home."

Mandie sighed, followed her, and said, "All right, come on into the house with us, then. We'll find something to do." She looked back and saw Jonathan and Joe exchange grins.

As the group stepped onto the front porch, they stopped to shake the snow off their coats and hats, then they went inside. Mandie put Snowball down, and he raced off in the direction of the kitchen. She placed her box on the shelf under a table near the front door.

They hung their wraps on the hall tree, and Mandie looked through the doorway to the parlor. The adults were gathered around the fireplace.

"Mother, we're back. It's beginning to snow," Mandie said.

"All right, dear, just don't go back out in it," Elizabeth told her absent-mindedly as she continued her conversation with the others in the parlor.

"I have an idea," Mandie said, looking at Jonathan. "Let's go to the kitchen, and I'll introduce you to everybody. You said you wanted to meet all the servants."

"I sure do, after all I've heard about them from you," Jonathan agreed.

"We might even manage to get a piece of that chocolate cake that was on the table at noon," Joe said with a big grin.

"Sounds delicious," Jonathan agreed.

"Or maybe a cup of hot cocoa like we had last

night when we decorated your tree," Polly added.

"Come on," Mandie said, leading the way down the corridor. "I'm sure Aunt Lou will be glad to oblige."

When she pushed the door to the kitchen, Mandie found all the servants gathered around the kitchen table, drinking coffee and snacking.

"We're just in time," she said to her friends as they all entered the kitchen. Then looking at Aunt Lou, she said, "This is my friend Jonathan Guyer from New York, and he wanted to meet you all."

Aunt Lou stood up and said, "Well, now, we'll all be pleased to meet your friend, but whut do you say we do dis over cake and coffee?" She smiled at Mandie.

"You are always a step ahead of me," Mandie said, laughing. "That's exactly what we were saying on the way in here—chocolate cake and coffee or cocoa."

"Well, don't jes' stand der, my chile," Aunt Lou said as she went toward the stove. "Make places fo' yo' friends at de table. Liza, you git de cups and plates."

The servants moved over and made room for the young people at the table, and Jonathan looked around at the friendly faces and was surprised to be welcomed into the kitchen. As he sat down, he remarked to Mandie, "You know, at my house we aren't allowed in the kitchen. This is a wonderful atmosphere here."

Mandie smiled as she sat next to Joe, and Polly managed to get next to Jonathan. "I know all about those high and mighty servants your father has up there in New York," she said. "But down here we're all like one big family."

"Mandie and I have eaten here in this kitchen before," Joe said to Jonathan. "And at my house we have Mr. and Mrs. Miller who live in a tenant house on my father's land and do work for my mother in the house. So you see, this is why I wouldn't want to go to college in New York. Nobody is anybody's friend up there, and down here everybody knows everybody and treats them as a friend."

"Then maybe someday I'll come down south to live," Jonathan remarked.

As soon as everyone had been introduced and coffee and hot cocoa and chocolate cake had been served, Jonathan became the center of attention and was asked a lot of questions about New York, that faraway land where these servants had never been. He told them about the city and his home, and when he started naming all of the servants, everybody gasped.

"How kin you find work fo' all dem people to do?" Aunt Lou asked.

"I suppose they all find something to do," Jonathan replied as he began eating the chocolate cake on his plate.

"I'm sure they do," Mandie said. "Aunt Lou, his house is enormous. You can get lost in it and not find your way out for days."

Jonathan laughed and said, "It's not that bad. We don't use the whole house."

Liza had been silently listening to every word spoken, and now she said, "We'se got part of dis heah house closed off, too."

Mandie looked at her, wondering what she meant. "Well, we have guest rooms upstairs that are very seldom used," she said to Jonathan.

"But, Missy 'Manda, dat ain't all," Liza reminded her. "You knows dat dark tunnel place nobody don't wanna go in."

"Oh, the secret tunnel. I'm glad you mentioned that, Liza," Mandie said. Turning to Jonathan, she said, "We'll show you the secret tunnel if you'd like."

"The secret tunnel?" Jonathan questioned. "You have a secret tunnel?"

"Oh yes, my ancestors built it under this house to hide the Cherokee people during the time the government was forcing them to leave this part of the country," Mandie reminded him. "Don't you remember my telling you that I'm part Cherokee?"

"I remember you telling me that you're part Cherokee, but I'm not sure you ever told me about the tunnel, but let's go. I'd like to see it," Jonathan replied.

"I'll get a lantern," Joe said as he rose from the table. Everyone else stood up.

"And don't forget plenty of matches," Mandie reminded him.

"Mandie, are you really going into that tunnel?" Polly asked.

"Sure, Polly," Mandie said. "You don't have to go with us if you don't want to."

Polly glanced at Jonathan, who was watching her. "I'll go, but let's don't stay in there too long," she finally agreed.

As the group started to leave the kitchen, everyone thanked the servants, and Mandie looked at Liza and asked, "Don't you want to come with us, Liza?" She leaned closer and whispered, "You could take care of Polly if she gets scared."

"No, no, Missy 'Manda, I ain't wantin' to go in

dat place, nevuh!'' Liza said, backing away from her.

Joe had been listening and now he teased, ''Liza, one of these days we're going to take you for a walk all the way through the tunnel.''

Liza's eyes got big and she rushed across the kitchen away from the young people. ''Ain't nuthin' gwine take me in dat dark place,'' she said.

Jonathan smiled at her and said, ''If it's all that bad, I might get scared, too. Don't you want to go? We could always come right back out.''

''No, no, no!'' Liza said as she stood by the big iron cookstove, rubbing her hands together.

''All right, Liza, we'll see you when we come back, then,'' Mandie told the girl as the group left the room.

Chapter 9 / A Scary Ordeal

As the four young people stepped into the hall-way from the kitchen, Mandie said, "Joe, while you get the lantern I'll ask Uncle John if he'll open his office and we can go into the tunnel from there."

"Then y'all meet me at the top of the staircase on the third floor," Joe said, turning to go out the back door from the hallway to the porch.

"All right," Mandie called back to him as she led the way to the parlor. She spoke from the doorway since her uncle and Lindall Guyer were sitting nearby with Dr. Woodard. "Uncle John, would it be possible to get you to unlock your office? We want to show Jonathan the secret tunnel, and it would be easier if we could go straight down from there."

"If you promise not to light the candles up there," John Shaw said, smiling as he rose. "Your mother is always afraid they will start a fire, you know."

Lindall Guyer also stood up. "A secret tunnel? In this house?" he asked.

"Do you want to go with us, Mr. Guyer?" Mandie asked.

"Not this time," Mr. Guyer replied. "Maybe later."

"I'll explain all about this tunnel when I come back. I'll run up and unlock the door for them," John Shaw said.

Mandie saw her uncle pull his keys out of his pocket as he went ahead of them up the stairs. Everyone knew his office was kept locked and that the key stayed in a secret hiding place in his and Elizabeth's bedroom. So Mandie wondered why he had the key in his pocket.

The three young people followed John Shaw up the staircase and found Joe waiting at the top with a lantern in his hand. John Shaw looked at the lantern and said, "Please be careful with that lantern. I know you have to have one to go through the tunnel, but please be very careful."

"Yes, sir, I will," Joe promised.

John Shaw led the way down the long corridor to his office and unlocked the door. As he pushed it open he said, "It would be much safer if you would just light the lamps in here and not touch the candles, even though I know you would like to show Jonathan how they work, Amanda. Maybe when his father comes up later we could light the candles." He went into the room and walked over to a small door in the corner, which he unlocked.

"We won't touch them, Uncle John," Mandie promised as he left the room. Turning back to Jonathan, who was standing in the doorway as Joe lit the lamps, she said, "The candles work like magic.

They are so close together that if you light one, the one next to it will catch, and the next one, and so on around the room.''

Jonathan stepped inside the room and looked at the candles in the wall sconces close together around three sides of the room, with shelves above and below them holding hundreds of books. ''I never saw so many candles before,'' he said.

Joe stopped by the huge desk in front of a large stained-glass window and touched a lighted match to the lamp sitting there.

Jonathan looked around the room and asked, ''Well, where is the secret tunnel?''

Mandie walked over to the small door in the corner that her uncle had unlocked and said, ''You can go in through here.'' She opened the door as Jonathan came over to watch.

''But that's just a paneled wall inside,'' Jonathan said.

''Oh, but watch this,'' Mandie said as she reached in a corner of the paneling and pressed a latch. The paneled wall swung open, revealing steps inside.

Joe stepped inside first with the lantern. Mandie waved Jonathan in behind him and then turned to Polly, who had been in the tunnel before. ''You're next, Polly,'' Mandie said.

Polly stood at the doorway and hesitated.

''Well, aren't you going with us?'' Mandie asked.

''I . . . I suppose so,'' Polly finally agreed as she stepped inside. ''But I do think we should have brought two lanterns just in case the one Joe has goes out.''

Mandie followed her and replied, ''But Joe has

plenty of matches to re-light the lantern if it goes out."

"This is very interesting," Jonathan remarked as they came to the bottom of the short flight of steps. Joe flashed the lantern around, showing a small room.

"This is only the beginning," Mandie told him.

"And we not only go all the way down through the house," Joe said. "The tunnel goes under the ground for a long distance, too."

"If you remember, we started on the third floor, but the tunnel also goes on up to the attic," Mandie explained.

"It sure took an intelligent architect to build this," Jonathan remarked. "You said it was designed when the house was built, didn't you?"

"Right," Mandie said.

"Watch your step, now," Joe warned. "We're going ahead and there's more steps."

"I'm right behind you," Jonathan said.

Joe led them down more steps, through more little rooms, platforms, and doors. After a while he stopped again to swing the lantern around in a dark room full of furniture.

"Furniture in here?" Jonathan questioned.

"Sure," Mandie said. "Don't forget, my Cherokee kinpeople actually lived in this tunnel while the government was trying to move all of them out of North Carolina."

"Looks like handmade furniture," Jonathan said, examining a bench nearby as they stood in the middle of the small room.

"It is, all of it," Mandie said.

"Mandie and I accidentally discovered this tunnel," Polly said. "We bumped into a paneled wall upstairs. It opened up and we got caught behind it when it closed. It was scary."

"I imagine it was," Jonathan said. Then he looked at Mandie in the dim light and asked, "Do you mean your family didn't know this was here? Your current family?"

"Uncle John knew about it, and he was the one who told us the whole history. It was just Polly and me who didn't know it was here until we more or less fell into it," Mandie said with a smile.

"Shall we go on?" Joe asked.

"You mean there's more ahead?" Jonathan asked.

"Yes, that is if we can find the way out of here," Joe teased. He began swinging the lantern around. "Anybody see a door or steps or anything to get out of this room?"

"Oh, Joe is just teasing," Mandie started to say when suddenly everything went black. "Joe, what happened?" she quickly asked as she felt Polly grab hold of her arm.

"The lantern went out," Joe said.

"Well, for goodness' sakes, re-light it," Mandie said.

"Oh, I can't see anything," Polly said in a trembling voice.

"I'm not afraid, but how are we going to see to get out of here, with all those steps and doors?" Jonathan asked nearby.

"Y'all just wait a minute. I'm trying to find a match," Joe said.

"Don't tell me you didn't bring any matches," Mandie said. She was beginning to get nervous, too, but she tried to hide it.

"Of course I brought matches. Only I can't seem

to find them," Joe said. "I know I put them in the pocket of my jacket here."

"We'll never get out of here in one piece," Polly moaned as she held tightly to Mandie's arm. "I can just feel all kinds of squirmy things running across my feet and hanging over my head. Oh-h-h-h!"

Mandie was beginning to feel the same way, but she was not about to admit it. She shook Polly's hand real hard and said loudly, "Polly, stop it! We've been in here in the dark before, and we got out."

"I sure hope someone knows the way in the dark," Joe finally spoke. "I've lost the matches."

"Lost the matches?" Jonathan, Mandie, and Polly all spoke at once.

"Sorry, but I have a hole in my pocket that I didn't know about when I put the matches in here," Joe explained.

"You mean you've been dropping matches all the way down through the tunnel?" Mandie asked. "Oh, Joe, that could be dangerous. We need to get out of here and get another light and find all those matches. A rat could spark one and burn the house up."

"I'm sorry," Joe replied. "Right now I think we'd do better to keep on going down rather than going back up because I believe we are nearer to the entrance in the woods."

"All right," Mandie agreed. "Now, if we could just all hold on to the next one in line as we move on, maybe we won't fall down if we miss a step."

"Good idea," Jonathan agreed. "If Joe will go first, I'll move back and be last. That way we can protect the girls between us."

Mandie felt Jonathan move behind her in the dark, and she reached to hold his hand. "Polly, give me your hand and give the other one to Joe," she said as she tried to see in the darkness of the room. She felt Polly grasp her hand. "Now while we are holding hands and before we move on, let's just say our verse." She paused, and then together the group repeated her favorite verse, " 'What time I am afraid I will put my trust in Thee.' "

Mandie took a deep breath and said, "I'm ready."

"Then we'd better get going," Joe said.

"Yes, let's get going," Jonathan answered.

"Right," Polly said in a shaky voice.

"I'm ready," Mandie added. "But please go slow, Joe."

"Don't worry, I will," he replied.

They moved forward, and eventually Joe announced that they were approaching steps down. The group slowed down, and Mandie found herself putting one foot forward to feel where she was going each time she made a step. No one was talking much except for an occasional "oh," "ah," or "watch out for a step."

Then Jonathan spoke. "Just think what an adventure I'll have to talk about when I return home to New York. My father's servants will never believe this," he said with a laugh.

"That is, if you are able to return, Jonathan," Polly said. "This could cause an accident if we aren't careful."

"I apologize," Joe said. "I'll never volunteer to carry the lantern or the matches again."

"It could have happened to any of us," Mandie said. "The only thing I'm really worried about is coming back with a light and finding all those matches you lost."

"One thing about it," Joe said as they slowly moved on, "we know I lost them during our walk in the upper half of the tunnel."

They finally stepped down into a hallway that Mandie knew led to the outside door of the tunnel.

"The door is straight ahead," Mandie told the others.

Joe moved on and the others followed until he said, "This is it. Now I have to find the key to the door here."

"It's supposed to be on the nail on the left-hand side of the door," Mandie told him as they all broke the line and came crowding around Joe.

"I haven't located the nail yet," Joe replied.

Mandie moved up beside him and began feeling around the wall. "I've got it," she exclaimed as her hand touched the big metal key and she took it down from the wall. Stooping down she moved her hands around until she felt the doorknob and then located the keyhole beneath.

"Mandie, please hurry," Polly begged.

"I'm hurrying, Polly," Mandie said as she tried to insert the key in the keyhole in the darkness of the corridor. Finally, it slipped into the slot and she turned the lock.

"Here, I'll help you," Joe said as he reached to assist her in pulling open the heavy metal door.

As soon as the door swung open and they could see daylight, they all began laughing and hugging one another.

"Now all we have to do is get one more lantern and a whole lot of matches and go back and look for those matches that Joe lost," Mandie told them. She stepped outside and said, "It isn't snowing anymore."

The others followed her, and Jonathan looked around in amazement. "You mean that tunnel came all the way down here in these woods?" he asked.

"It sure did," Mandie replied. "So now we have to go through the woods and up to the house and start all over again in the tunnel."

"Oh, it's cold out here," Polly complained, shivering as the wind blew. They didn't know they were going to be outside, so they didn't wear coats.

"It's not far to the house. We'll just have to hurry," Mandie told them.

When they reached the house, they went straight to the parlor. The adults were still there talking.

"Uncle John, I think I'd better let you know what we're doing," Mandie began as the four stood in the doorway.

"Oh, y'all are back," John Shaw said as he looked at them.

"We're back, but we've got to go again," Mandie replied, and she explained what had happened. "So you see, we have to go back inside the tunnel and try to find all those matches."

"Yes, by all means," John Shaw said. "And please don't be gone too long this time."

"We won't," Mandie promised as she looked across at her mother and grandmother, who were busy conversing with Mrs. Woodard. She turned back to her friends and said, "Let's get going."

They went to the back porch, picked up another lantern, checked both lanterns to be sure they were full of fuel, and then got matches from the pantry. This time Mandie put some in her pocket as Joe took a few.

They reentered the tunnel and began searching

for the lost matches. With the light from the two lanterns, it was easier going this time, and the extra light made it easy to spot the matches. By the time they reached the spot where the lantern had gone out, they had found all the matches Joe said he had been carrying.

"I suppose we can go back now," Polly said.

"Oh no, I just thought of something," Mandie said as they started to go back up. "We have to go all the way to the outside door at the end of the tunnel in order to lock it. I put the key back on the nail when we went outside down there."

"Unless y'all want to go around through the woods and lock it from the outside," Joe suggested.

Mandie thought for a moment and said, "No, that won't work because there wouldn't be a key inside for anyone to get out if they happen to go down from in here."

"If you girls want to wait here, I can run down with Joe and lock it," Jonathan offered. "Since I don't know the way, he would have to go, too."

"Oh no!" Polly immediately objected. "I'd be afraid to stay here with just Mandie."

"There's nothing to be afraid of," Mandie told her.

"But the lantern could go out again," Polly reminded her.

"All right, then," Mandie said, looking at the boys. "One of you come with me and I'll lock the door. The other one of you can stay here with Polly."

"I'll go," Joe said. "I can move faster than Jonathan because he doesn't know the way."

"That's fine," Mandie said, handing her lantern to Jonathan. "Here, keep this lantern, and Joe can take his with us. We'll be right back. Please don't go away or move to another place."

"We won't," Jonathan promised as he took the lantern and he and Polly sat down.

Mandie smiled to herself as she went on down the tunnel with Joe. She couldn't wait to tell Liza about it because Liza had told her she thought Polly might be interested in Jonathan. Well, here was Polly's chance.

Joe led the way with the lantern, and he and Mandie hurried down to the outside door, locked it, placed the key back on the nail, and began their way back up.

"It has stopped snowing, and I don't believe it's time to eat yet," Mandie said. "Maybe we could go back out with the treasure map and see if we can figure any more of it out."

"I don't know what good we can do with that pile of dirt, but if you want to I'll go with you," Joe said.

Mandie looked up at him in the dim lantern light and smiled. "I knew you would," she said.

"Well, I'm not so sure Jonathan and Polly will want to go," Joe told her as he held the lantern higher to light the steps they were going up.

"Jonathan will probably go along just for the fun of it, and Polly will probably go along just because Jonathan is going," Mandie said with another smile.

Joe looked back at her as they climbed the steps and said, "Do you think Polly is interested in Jonathan?"

"Maybe," Mandie answered.

So when they reached Jonathan and Polly and continued on up the tunnel with them, Mandie asked, "Would y'all be interested in going back outside with Joe and me and the treasure map?"

They had reached the top and came out in John

Shaw's office. Mandie turned to look at them.

Jonathan shrugged and said, "If you want to, it's all right with me."

"Well, I suppose I could go for a little while," Polly said, looking at Jonathan.

"All right, then. As soon as we check in with Uncle John and get our coats, we'll go outside," Mandie said.

They hurried down the stairs and let John Shaw know they were back and had found the matches.

"Now we're going outside for a little while," Mandie told him. Her mother was still engrossed in conversation with the other women.

"Don't be gone too long," John Shaw told her. "We will be eating a little early tonight since we are going over to Mrs. Cornwallis's house afterwards to help decorate her tree, remember."

"We won't be gone long," Mandie promised.

The four of them put on their coats and hats, then Mandie picked up the box and they left the house.

Chapter 10 / This and That,
Here and There

Mandie led the others in a different direction this time with the stuff in the box. At the front gate they went right instead of left as they had done previously, but nothing seemed to fit the indentations in the dirt in the box, and her friends soon lost interest. Even Snowball, who had followed them at the beginning, drifted off on his own.

They all paused at an intersection, and Mandie said with disappointment in her voice, "Maybe these little marks represent roads or paths through the woods. We may be in the wrong place altogether."

Her three friends just nodded and looked at her. She knew they were tired of the game, but she couldn't think of anything else to do to entertain them.

Joe finally looked at her and said, "Maybe we

should just go on back for now. It's getting late."

"That's what I was thinking," Mandie agreed as she put the lid on the box. "We can try again tomorrow after we go buy those baskets."

They returned to the house and stopped by the parlor. Snowball followed them. The adults were still there, but this time Elizabeth saw them and said, "Amanda, I think you should all go up to your rooms and freshen up now. Supper will soon be ready."

"Yes, ma'am," Mandie agreed as she placed the box on the table in the parlor where she had left it yesterday.

"Polly, you are welcome to stay and eat supper with us if you like," Elizabeth told the girl, who had stood there at the doorway undecided whether to take off her coat and hat.

"Thank you, Mrs. Shaw, but I suppose I'd better go home," Polly replied. "I'd much rather stay and eat with y'all, but I know Mother will be expecting me back for supper because we have company, you know."

"Then please tell your mother we will all be over after a while," Elizabeth said.

"Yes, ma'am, I will," Polly said, going back out into the hallway. "Mandie, Joe, and Jonathan, I'll see y'all over at my house."

"Right," Joe called after her.

"See you then," Jonathan said.

"All right, Polly," Mandie told her.

Polly went out the front door. Mandie turned to the boys and said, "I'll see you both back down here for supper. I've got to go to the kitchen for something right now."

"Sure," Jonathan said.

"Right," Joe told her.

Mandie watched until the two boys disappeared up the staircase, then she went on down the hallway to the kitchen. As she pushed the door open, she found Liza helping Aunt Lou warm up the leftovers from the noon meal for supper, which was the usual practice on Sunday.

"Dat white cat dun eatin' his suppuh," Liza told her as she pointed to Snowball happily gobbling up food scraps on a plate by the cookstove.

Mandie laughed and said, "I knew he would get served first." She walked over near Liza, who was getting dishes down from the cupboard. Aunt Lou was on the far side of the huge room moving things around on the cookstove. Cupping her hand over the side of her mouth, she whispered, "I left Polly alone with Jonathan in the tunnel."

Liza's eyes got big and she said, "Missy 'Manda, you dun lef' dem in de tunnel! How dey gwine git out?" She paused in her work to look at Mandie.

"They're out," Mandie told her in a low voice. "You see, Joe and I had to go back down to the outside door and lock it, so we left Polly and Jonathan in that room about halfway up that has all that furniture in it, and then we all came back out together."

"Uh-huh," Liza said, smiling. "Wonder whut dem two had to say to each other whilst dey alone."

"I don't know, but you thought if Polly had a chance she would get interested in Jonathan, so I gave her a chance," Mandie replied. She glanced at Aunt Lou, who didn't seem to be listening.

"Well," Liza said, "I dun tole you if dat don't wark, den voodoo spell—"

"Liza!" Aunt Lou yelled so loud even Mandie

jumped. "I dun tole you I ain't puttin' up wid you usin' dat word round heah, and I sho' don't mean mebbe. Next time I heahs you say dat word, I'se gwine wash out yo' mouth and shut you up in de tunnel fo' a week."

Liza was so frightened she was almost trembling as she replied, "But, Aunt Lou, dat word you talkin' 'bout was my kinpeople's religion way back 'fo I was bawn, and dey was kin to me, so dat word be my religion, too."

Aunt Lou immediately dropped a lid on the pot she was checking on and hurried across the room to stand firmly in front of Liza. "I said you ain't gwine use dat word, and you ain't gwine talk 'bout dat word no mo'. We'se Christian people, and dat word ain't no Christian word, and it ain't nevuh been yo' religion, either. You'se Christian, and you'se gwine stay Christian."

Liza had moved back a step and was hugging herself with her arms and staring at the floor.

Aunt Lou moved a step nearer to the girl and said, "Liza, I'm talkin' to you. You looks at me when I talks to you, you heah?"

"Yessum," Liza said in a low voice as she ventured to look up at the woman.

"I dun raised you myself, and I expects you to listen to me when I talks to you," Aunt Lou continued. "Now, I wants to know where you git dat word, anyhow."

Liza shuffled her feet and nervously answered, "Dat girl whut come visit dat Cornwallises' cook, she dun tole me 'bout dat word last week. Dat's where I git de word."

"If I ketches you sayin' dat word agin den I be gwine over fo' a talk wid dat cook. Now, you git on wid yo' work," Aunt Lou said.

Although Aunt Lou had not even looked directly at Mandie during this conversation with Liza, Mandie had gradually edged her way over to the door and now she slipped out into the hallway without a word. Aunt Lou was angry. Mandie had never seen the old woman so upset, and she didn't want anything to do with it all. She hoped Liza obeyed Aunt Lou because she sounded like she meant that threat of shutting Liza up in the tunnel.

Mandie hurried upstairs to her room, washed up, and changed her clothes. She thought about the confrontation between Aunt Lou and Liza the whole time she was getting ready for supper. Maybe Liza didn't understand what voodoo was and needed to learn something about it in order to realize it was, as Aunt Lou had said, not Christian. Mandie didn't know that much about it, and she didn't think she could help Liza, but she would try to think of someone who could.

When Mandie got back down to the parlor, the boys were already there and to her surprise they were sitting near each other and talking. The only other person in the room was her grandmother, who was seated in a chair by the fireplace.

"Amanda, dear, come sit by me," Mrs. Taft said as she looked up to see Mandie come into the room.

Mandie smiled as she walked past Joe and Jonathan and pulled up a footstool by her grandmother's chair. "Are you going with us later over to Polly's house?" Mandie asked as she sat down.

"Yes, I suppose I'll have to, Mrs. Cornwallis being your mother's neighbor and all," Mrs. Taft replied. "Things have been moving so fast since we got here that I'd really rather stay here and catch my breath, but it's Christmastime and there's always so much to do."

"I know what you mean, Grandmother," Mandie said. "And everybody gets all wound up, and sometimes there are words spoken that should not have been."

Mrs. Taft quickly looked at her and asked, "Why, Amanda, have you been having words with someone, dear?"

"No, Grandmother, it was Liza and Aunt Lou," Mandie replied, and then she suddenly had an idea. "Liza needs someone to talk to her and explain things, and I believe you are the right person to do this. I know she looks up to you."

"What on earth are you talking about, Amanda?" the lady asked.

Mandie went on to explain the events concerning voodoo. "I know Aunt Lou is trying to teach Liza, but she doesn't give any explanation or anything. I'm afraid Liza doesn't understand the reason why she shouldn't believe in that stuff. She doesn't really know what it is, I don't think. And I believe if you talked to her she would listen to everything you say."

"Well, I certainly don't want to interfere with Aunt Lou's authority over Liza," Mrs. Taft said.

"But you wouldn't be. You would actually be helping Aunt Lou out because she is not educated enough to know how to handle this," Mandie said. Then looking up at the lady with her blue eyes, she added, "Please, Grandmother?"

"I suppose . . . if the right opportunity presents itself I could talk to Liza. I'll see," Mrs. Taft promised.

"Thank you, Grandmother," Mandie said,

reaching to squeeze the lady's hand. Grinning up at her, she added, "You know, it's a pity you were born rich because you would have made a good teacher."

"Amanda!" Mrs. Taft exclaimed. "I would never have the patience with unruly children to teach them anything."

Elizabeth and Mrs. Woodard came into the parlor then, with John Shaw, Dr. Woodard, and Lindall Guyer right behind them.

"I've just checked with Aunt Lou, and I believe she's ready for us to go into the dining room," Elizabeth said as she looked around the room.

Everyone rose and followed her into the dining room. They hurried through the meal and then went over to Polly's house.

The young people did most of the decorating. Mandie noticed that Mrs. Cornwallis and her visiting relatives seemed more interested in carrying on a conversation with the other adults than putting up a Christmas tree. Also, the Cornwallises' servants were not invited to join in as John Shaw's had been. And Polly followed every move Jonathan made. He kept glancing at Mandie and smiling behind Polly's back.

Mandie was glad when it was finally time to go home and go to bed. She was tired. It had been a long day.

But then the next day was a long day, too. So many people and so many things going on.

As soon as breakfast was over, Elizabeth suggested going downtown to purchase the baskets, and everybody wanted to go. It turned out to be time consuming just trying to keep up with everyone, but Christmas spirit filled the air. Carolers were on street corners. The children's school choir was singing on the steps of the courthouse. Now and then Mandie noticed a shopper joining in the songs. And a few snowflakes fell, glistening on the town's street decorations and then fading away.

"This is all so different from Christmastime in New York," Jonathan remarked as he walked along with Mandie, Joe, and Polly, who were trying to keep up with the adults. "It seems more personal somehow, more real."

"This is only the second Christmas I've been here in Franklin," Mandie told him. "I was raised in the country in Swain County, you know, and things were different there, too. There were a lot more things going on at people's houses and at the school and at the church." She leaned forward to look up at Joe, who was on the far side of their group. "You still live there, Joe. You know how it is."

"Yes, it's not as convenient to go into Bryson City and shop as it is to live in Franklin and just walk downtown," he said with a smile.

Jonathan looked at Joe and said, "I'd like to visit your part of the country sometime. I'm not especially what you'd call a city person. I suppose I've lived in so many cities, going to school and all that, that I'm tired of it."

Joe replied as they walked on, "You'd be welcome at our house any time you want to come visit."

Mandie smiled as she looked from one boy to the other and said, "I'm so glad."

Polly had been silent until now and she asked, "Glad about what?"

"Glad to know Joe and Jonathan have become

friends," Mandie answered.

"Well, we certainly aren't enemies," Jonathan said with a big grin.

"I hope not," Joe said, laughing.

As they continued along the street, Polly turned to Mandie again and asked, "Do you think I could come visit, too, when you go?"

"Of course, Polly. Remember, I own my father's house now, and although Mr. Smith lives in it to take care of it, I still would like to go see it for myself now and then," Mandie replied.

"But you always stay with us," Joe said.

"Yes, and you're going away to college next school year, so we'd better all try to get out there before then," Mandie reminded him.

"Maybe next summer when school is out," Jonathan suggested.

"That would be a good time to come see us," Joe said.

The adults had finally found the baskets for sale and stopped to purchase some. An old woman in a stand on the corner across from the courthouse had the ones made by the Cherokee people.

"Amanda, these are the baskets Uncle Ned brought in," Elizabeth told Mandie as she examined the piles of merchandise.

"I would like to take some back for Miss Prudence and Miss Hope at my school," Mandie said. "And I'd also like one for myself. And I must get one for Celia, too."

"Now, wait a minute," Jonathan teased. "You can't buy them all because I want some, too." He began sorting through the pile.

Lindall Guyer inspected the baskets and said, "I must buy some of these for some friends back in

New York. I'm sure they've never seen baskets handmade by the Cherokee Indians." He reached to pick one up.

Mrs. Woodard decided she wanted one for a bread basket, even though the Woodards had been longtime friends of the Cherokee people and had bought such things from them before.

Everyone ended up with baskets to carry, but they came in handy as containers for other purchases they made along the way.

When they returned to the house, Liza opened the front door for them. Mrs. Taft was the last adult to enter, and Mandie heard her speak to Liza.

"I wonder if you could come up to my room for a few minutes, Liza," Mrs. Taft told the young girl.

Liza looked at her in surprise and said, "If it take long, I has to ax Aunt Lou, 'cause she dun give me work to do."

"Of course, ask Aunt Lou," Mrs. Taft told her. "I'll be in my room." She went down the hallway to the stairs.

"Yessum," Liza said, looking after the lady. "I go ax."

Mandie smiled to herself. She knew why her grandmother had asked Liza to go to her room. Maybe she would be able to make Liza understand things.

"What are we up to now?" Joe asked as he came down the hallway behind Mandie.

Mandie stopped to turn around and look at him, and Jonathan and Polly, who were following. "Would anyone be interested in going off in a different direction for the treasure map in the box?"

"Sure, I'd be interested in seeing everything while I'm here," Jonathan told her. "Anywhere you want to go is fine with me."

"Her uncle John owns a lot of territory around here," Polly said.

"He even owns a ruby mine," Joe added.

"Really? I've never seen a mine of any kind," Jonathan said, looking at Mandie.

"The Burnses, Ludie and Jake, they live on Uncle John's property, and Jake takes care of the mines. Uncle John has several mines. Jake could tell you all about them," Mandie said as they still stood in the hallway.

"But I'd rather you show them to me," Jonathan said.

"I can show you the ruby mine, but the others are too far off," Mandie said. "Let's go to our rooms and get rid of all these packages first." She started toward the staircase.

"I'll be back in five minutes," Joe said.

"I'll go up with you, Mandie," Polly said, following Mandie.

"I'll see you all in the parlor," Jonathan said.

They all hurried up the stairs and to their different rooms to deposit the things they had bought.

Mandie found Snowball asleep on her bed. She quickly put her packages in the bottom of the wardrobe and closed the doors. Then she looked at Polly and said, "Maybe you'd better put your things in here with mine. Snowball has a bad habit of tearing up packages sometimes." She reopened the doors, and Polly added her purchases.

"Don't you think Jonathan is interesting?" Polly asked as she picked up a hairbrush on Mandie's dresser, removed her hat, and began brushing her hair.

"Of course," Mandie agreed. "I'd better let

Mother know where we're going. Are you ready?"

Polly quickly laid down the brush and put her hat back on. "I'm ready," she said, following Mandie out the door.

Mandie stopped by her mother's room to say they were taking Jonathan around the property, and Elizabeth reminded her to be back in time for the noon meal.

As the two girls went along the corridor toward the staircase, they met up with Jonathan and Joe.

"Supposed to meet us in the parlor," Mandie teased as she and Polly walked on.

"Right," Joe said with a laugh as he raced ahead and down the stairs.

Jonathan quickly followed him.

Then as Mandie and Polly started down they met Liza.

The young girl stopped Mandie on the steps. "Missy 'Manda, yo' grandmama, she want me up to huh room," she said.

"Then you'd better go on, Liza," Mandie said with a smile.

"She ain't nevuh axed me to come up special to huh room," Liza said, still standing there.

"Maybe it's something special she wants you to do," Mandie suggested. "We have to go on, Liza. Joe and Jonathan are waiting for us in the parlor."

Liza looked from Mandie to Polly and back again as she said, "Where you be gwine dis heah time?"

"All around. Jonathan wants to see everything," Mandie said.

Liza looked serious as she said, "Don't be forgittin' 'bout de graveyard, Missy 'Manda."

"The graveyard?" Mandie answered. "Oh, of course, we'll go over to the cemetery so I can show him my little brother's grave. He knows about him. Thanks for reminding me."

"I'd rather go wid y'all than up to see yo' grandmama," Liza said.

Mandie laughed and said, "Liza, you'd better go on and see what my grandmother wants. She doesn't like to be kept waiting." She went ahead down the stairs.

"Guess I have to," Liza said as she went on up the steps.

Mandie laughed as she and Polly walked on toward the parlor.

"Why is Liza afraid of your grandmother, Mandie?" Polly asked.

"I don't think she's exactly afraid of Grandmother. She just believes my grandmother is somebody extra special because of all her money and jewels and everything," Mandie said.

"But I've always heard that your uncle John is the richest man this side of Richmond, and Liza isn't afraid of him," Polly told her.

Mandie laughed again. "That's because she was born and raised right here in this house," she said.

They came to the door of the parlor, and Joe and Jonathan quickly left the room to join them in the hallway. They were ready to go anywhere.

Mandie thought of Liza again. She hoped her grandmother could make the girl understand why Aunt Lou had been so angry with her.

Chapter 11 / More Company

Mandie could hardly sleep that night because she knew Uncle Ned, Sallie, and Morning Star would be arriving the next day, which was Christmas Eve, and she prayed it would not snow so they could get over the mountain. She thought about the box with the dirt in it. So far she had not been able to solve anything regarding that, but when Sallie got there, Mandie was sure she would help.

Jonathan had enjoyed the walk around Uncle John's property, and Mandie thought that since he and Joe had become friends, maybe Joe would entertain him so she could slip off with Sallie. She drifted off to sleep trying to figure out how she would do that.

A loud metallic noise woke Mandie. She quickly sat up and looked around. Liza was working on the fire, so it must be morning already. She felt as though she had slept for only a few minutes.

"Morning, Liza," Mandie greeted the young girl,

pushing up her pillows and stretching under the quilts. She nudged Snowball off the bed, and he jumped down to join Liza in the warmth of the fire.

"Mawnin', Missy 'Manda. Sorry I dropped de shovel. Must woke you up," Liza said, poking the logs.

"That's all right, Liza. Must be time to get up if you're in here building up the fire," Mandie replied. "Did you go see my grandmother yesterday? I haven't had a chance to see you since then."

Liza jumped up, wiped her hands on her white apron, ran over to the bed, and plopped down near Mandie. "I hopes de Lawd blesses you, Missy 'Manda, 'cause you dun saved my soul from de devil, that you have," Liza started talking fast. "Miz Grandmama, she tell me all 'bout de devil puttin' dat voodoo stuff in my haid. I didn't knows dat voodoo belongs to him. But I knows now. Dis heah is de last time I'll ever talk about that bad word. Miz Grandmama, she know all 'bout it, but you see, Aunt Lou, she don't know all Miz Grandmama know."

Mandie reached to squeeze the girl's hand. "Oh, Liza, I'm so glad you understand now why Aunt Lou was so angry with you. It was all for your good," she said. Then she grinned mischievously and added, "Now Aunt Lou won't have to wash out your mouth and shut you up in the tunnel."

Liza jumped up, ran to the fireplace, and began spitting into the fire. Then she turned back to Mandie, smiled, and said, "There, I dun cleaned out my mouth." She picked up the bucket she carried to work on the fireplace every morning. "I has to go now. When you sees Miz Grandmama, you tells huh

I'm dun cured." She danced around the room and went to open the door.

"I'll be sure to tell her, Liza," Mandie called after her as she went into the hallway and closed the door behind her.

"Thank the Lord!" Mandie said with a big smile. She jumped up, took clothes out of the wardrobe, and began dressing in front of the heat from the fireplace. Looking down at Snowball, who was washing his face, she said, "Sallie will be here today."

Suddenly she remembered it might have snowed during the night. She ran to the window and pulled back the curtain. The sun wasn't shining, but it wasn't snowing, and there was no sign of any having fallen during the night. "Oh, it's going to be a wonderful day!" she exclaimed as she ran back to the fireplace to put on her shoes.

As soon as she had dressed, she hurried downstairs to the parlor. Snowball followed and went off in the direction of the kitchen. But no one was in the parlor when she got there. She must be the first one up this morning. However, by the time she sat down on a stool in front of the crackling fire, Joe came in.

"Good morning," they greeted each other.

Joe pulled up another stool and sat down near her. "Have you seen Jonathan?" he asked.

"Jonathan? No, I figured no one else was up," Mandie answered.

"I went by his room but he wasn't there, so I thought maybe he would be down here," Joe told her.

Mandie moved her feet to turn and look at Joe, and when she did she noticed a button was missing on one of her shoes. She looked around the floor. "Oh shucks! I've lost a button. See." She stuck her foot out for Joe to inspect it.

Joe stooped down and searched the floor. "You must have lost it before you came in here," he said as he stood up.

"These are not going to be very comfortable with them gaping open that way. I think I'll run back to my room and put on another pair," she said as she rose from the carpet.

"You have plenty of time. No one else seems to be up yet," Joe said.

Mandie stooped to look at the shoe. "I think I'll just take my shoes off to go up the steps," she said as she removed her shoes. "This one flops without the button."

Mandie hurried down the hallway and up the stairs to the second floor. She was about to go toward her room when she thought she heard someone coming down from the third floor. She stepped back and looked up. Jonathan was on the stairs above.

"Good morning," she called to him.

He stopped to look down through the stairwell. "Good morning," he said and came down to the landing. "Hope you don't mind. I got up early and was just browsing around. This is a fascinating house."

"Yes, it is," she agreed. She thought he looked guilty about something, but she couldn't think what.

"Did you forget to put on your shoes?" Jonathan asked with a big grin as he glanced at the shoes in her hand and her stockinged feet.

"Oh no, you see, I lost a button, and I have to go back to my room and put on another pair," she said, showing him the place where the missing button should have been. "Joe is in the parlor if you're looking for someone to talk to. And I'll be right back down." She started down the hallway.

"All right, the parlor it is," he replied as he continued down the staircase.

Mandie quickly found another pair of shoes in her room, put them on, and got back downstairs just as Uncle John, Dr. Woodard, and Mr. Guyer came in the front door.

"Y'all have already been out when I thought everyone was still in bed, except for Joe and Jonathan, that is," Mandie greeted them.

"We've been out for a walk. After all that sitting we did yesterday, I needed some exercise," Dr. Woodard told her as he hung his coat and hat on the hall tree.

"You young people have been doing a lot of walking so we thought we'd try it," John Shaw said.

"It's such beautiful country here that I'd like to stay outdoors as much as possible. Everything even smells so much better," Mr. Guyer added.

The men followed Mandie into the parlor. And soon thereafter everyone else had joined them and they went into the dining room for breakfast. The conversation centered around the expected arrival of Uncle Ned and his family and the possibility of snow.

"I'm sure they're on the way by now, and I haven't heard of any snow to amount to anything anywhere," Dr. Woodard said. "On our walk we stopped at the depot and spoke with the station master. He had not received any reports of snow."

"How do they travel when they come here to visit? I mean, do they take the train or what?" Jonathan asked.

Everyone around the table smiled at that question except Mr. Guyer. "They travel in a wagon, Jonathan," John Shaw said. "And in the winter they keep the top on it. There is no train where they live. And the road is more or less a rough trail through the mountain."

"Well, it certainly would be nice if somebody would get them a real road built, then," Jonathan replied. "Or build a railroad track over to where they live." He looked at his father.

Lindall Guyer smiled at his son and said, "I know exactly what you are thinking, that I have enough interest in railroad stock to use my influence to get this done. It would probably cost a fortune, and the railroad would have to have more passengers besides Uncle Ned and his family. However, I will think about it."

Mandie was thinking that both her grandmother and her uncle had the money to do such a thing, but she felt sure no one would finance such a deal.

"The Cherokee people might not patronize that kind of transportation," Joe said. "I think a good road would be a much better idea." And he looked at his father, then at John Shaw, and on to Mrs. Taft.

Mrs. Taft was the one who replied, "Someday. We'll see."

Mandie had very keen hearing and now she was sure she heard a wagon coming into their backyard. "Listen! Someone has come up outside," she said, looking around the table.

Liza suddenly came through the door and quickly went behind Mandie's chair and whispered, "Dat Injun man and his fambly is heah."

Mandie stood up and said, "Mother, please excuse me a minute. Liza said Uncle Ned has arrived."

"All right, but you come straight back here and finish your breakfast, and bring them with you," Elizabeth told Mandie, who was already leaving the room.

She ran to the back door and opened it. Sallie and Morning Star were getting down from the wagon as Uncle Ned held the reins. The girls met each other halfway and embraced.

"Y'all come on in. Mother says breakfast is waiting for y'all," Mandie told Sallie, who interpreted this into the Cherokee language for her grandmother, Morning Star.

Abraham, John Shaw's handyman, had also heard the wagon and came walking from his little house in the yard to help Uncle Ned unload the wagon and put away the horses.

"Soon I come in," the old Indian told Mandie.

As they all came into the dining room, Aunt Lou was scurrying around setting places for them at the table. Lindall Guyer and Jonathan had already met Uncle Ned in New York, and now the old man introduced his wife, Morning Star, and granddaughter, Sallie, as they all sat down.

"How did you get here so early?" John Shaw wanted to know.

"Leave sunup yesterday. Come over mountain. Sleep at house of friend Redbird. Come early. Maybe snow," the old man explained as the food was passed around the table.

"I'm so glad you came early, Uncle Ned," Elizabeth told him. "So we'll have more time to spend with y'all."

As the adults carried on their conversation,

Mandie and Sallie talked with Jonathan and Joe, who were sitting across the table from them. Mandie told Sallie about the strange gift she had received.

"On the outside it looked just like a present, but inside is all this dirt, twigs, and stuff. Just wait. I'll show you," Mandie explained.

"What is it supposed to be?" Sallie asked.

"Well," Mandie began as she looked at Joe. "It could be a treasure map, but if it is, I haven't been able to figure it out."

Sallie's black eyes widened as she said, "A treasure map would be interesting, but what treasure could it be?"

"A pile of dirt," Joe said jokingly.

"Joe, I'm going to prove to you that it's more than a pile of dirt," Mandie said. Then she turned to Sallie and asked, "Will you help me?"

Sallie shrugged and said, "I will do whatever I know how."

Mandie noticed Jonathan had not taken his eyes off the beautiful Indian girl since he had been introduced. And once in a while Sallie was cutting her eyes in his direction. Mandie smiled to herself. Jonathan had never met a real Cherokee girl. And Sallie had heard about Jonathan from Mandie after Mandie's trip to Europe with her grandmother where they had first met Jonathan. Mandie wondered what Polly would think about this.

"You young people should get a little rest this afternoon because we will be going to church at midnight tonight. This is Christmas Eve, remember," Elizabeth spoke from the foot of the table.

"Are we going out caroling tonight?" Mandie asked.

Elizabeth looked around the table and said, "Whoever wants to."

"Count me out. I can't sing a note," Lindall Guyer quickly said with a big smile.

To Mandie's amazement, Mrs. Taft immediately said, "Count me in. I believe I would enjoy doing that."

Mandie saw a look pass between the two people, and she wondered what it meant. So far she had not heard them say a single word to each other since Mr. Guyer had arrived.

"I'd like to go," Jonathan said. "I'm not very good at singing, but maybe everybody else will drown me out."

"Sallie, you've just got to go," Mandie told her. "You have to sing in Cherokee for us."

Sallie smiled and said, "I would be most honored to oblige."

"And of course you wouldn't be able to keep me from going," Joe said with a laugh.

The rest of the adults begged off.

"All right, Mother, that leaves you in charge," Elizabeth said.

"Fine," Mrs. Taft replied, and looking at the young people she said, "We'll just have us a good time."

And Mandie knew her grandmother meant it.

As soon as they finished with breakfast, Mandie showed the box to Sallie. The adults were all in the parlor, so the young people gathered in the sitting room at the back of the house.

"What does it look like to you?" Mandie asked as Sallie inspected the contents of the box.

Sallie thought for a moment and said, "Lots of dirt, twigs from a holly tree, also the red berries, small pieces of red ribbon, and tiny pebbles." She looked up at Mandie.

Mandie looked at Sallie and said, "What I meant was, does it look like a treasure map to you?"

Sallie bent over the box for a moment and then said, "There is a possibility it may be meant to be a treasure map. Those indentations may represent roads. However, these are small hills and valleys in them, and those look too sharp to be part of a roadway."

Mandie quickly looked to where Sallie pointed. She was right. The tiny ruts in the dirt that she assumed were roads might be something else. "Maybe a pathway through the woods?" she suggested.

"That is possible," Sallie agreed.

Mandie looked at Joe and Jonathan, who were listening to the conversation, and asked, "Would you all like to walk through the woods with us? We might be able to find these places down there."

"I suppose a little exercise wouldn't do us any harm," Joe said, rising from his chair.

"I'll go with you, too," Jonathan agreed.

Mandie noticed he was still staring at Sallie and that Sallie felt uncomfortable under his gaze.

"Let's get our coats, then," Mandie said.

All of them had to go to their rooms to get their coats and hats. Sallie was sharing Mandie's room, and her things had been put in there. Mandie told the boys they would meet them back at the foot of the staircase in five minutes, but she and Sallie took less than that to get theirs. As they rushed toward the steps to go down, Mandie saw Jonathan coming from the wrong end of the hallway. His room was down the other way. However, he had on his coat and hat.

"I . . . uh . . . got lost again. This is a big house, you know," he said as he quickly caught up with them.

Joe came hurrying from his room and said, "You mean you all beat me this time?"

"Slow poke," Mandie teased, but at the same time she wondered where Jonathan had been.

Mandie led the way outside and down through the woods. She and Sallie tried hard to relate the pathway to the indentations in the box. They looked at everything, discussed everything, and still couldn't decide what was what. Joe and Jonathan went along without any real interest.

They finally returned to the house an hour or so before the noon meal. The girls stayed in Mandie's room for a while discussing the possibilities of the stuff in the box. And then they talked about what they had been doing since they last saw each other. Mandie was relating the details of her visit to New York when there was a knock on the door.

"Come in," Mandie called across the room from where she and Sallie were sitting by the fireplace.

The door slowly opened, and Liza entered the room and closed the door behind her. "Oh, Missy 'Manda, I not know you has comp'ny in heah right now," she said.

"Liza, you know Sallie always stays in here with me when they come to visit," Mandie said.

"Well, uh, I jes' come back later," Liza said, turning to open the door.

"Wait, Liza," Mandie said. "What did you want to see me about?"

Liza looked at Sallie and then back to Mandie.

Then she said, "Missy 'Manda, I tells you later. Got to go now."

Mandie got up and walked across the room to the girl. "Liza, please tell me why you came in here," she said.

"Well, I guess it don't make no never mind, but I seen dat Yankee boy comin' down de steps from de attic jes' now," Liza said quickly in a loud whisper. "Whut he doin' up in de attic?"

Mandie frowned and said, "I don't know, Liza. Did he say anything to you?"

"Nope, I ducks fast in a door to one of dem rooms dat ain't used right now, and he didn't even see me," Liza explained.

"Where did he go then?" Mandie asked.

"He go straight in his room den," Liza said.

Mandie thought for a moment and then said, "I suppose he was just looking around. He said he wanted to see everything, so he probably meant the attic, too."

"I gots to go now fo' Aunt Lou be lookin' fo' me," Liza said, and she quickly slipped out the door and closed it.

"Is anything wrong?" Sallie asked. She had overheard the conversation.

"I don't think so," Mandie said, coming back to sit down. "I did see Jonathan coming down from the third floor today, so he might have been all the way up to the attic that time, too. I just can't imagine why he goes wandering off like that."

"Maybe he did just want to look around the house," Sallie suggested.

"I don't know, but it gives me a funny feeling somehow or other," Mandie said as she rose. "Come on. Let's go find him and Joe before Jonathan wanders off somewhere else."

They found the boys in the sitting room. Mandie wondered where Joe had been while Jonathan was strolling around upstairs. Liza didn't say she had seen Joe.

Joe looked up as the girls came into the room and asked, "What are we doing this afternoon?"

Mandie glanced at Sallie as they sat down and then said, "Whatever y'all would like to do." She looked at Jonathan.

"Do?" Jonathan repeated as he scratched his head. "I don't know. Why don't you show me the rest of your house, like the attic and the cellar?"

"The attic and the cellar?" Mandie questioned. "Do you really want to see the attic and the cellar?"

"Sure. Why not?" Jonathan said with a big grin.

"They are both dirty and smelly," Mandie said.

"That only makes them more interesting," Jonathan told her.

"Well, if you insist," Mandie finally agreed.

Snowball came into the room just then, and Joe said, "And, Mandie, please don't take that white cat with us. He'll get lost and we'll spend the rest of the day looking for him."

Snowball meowed loudly and jumped up on a chair and curled up.

"He could catch the rats if we see any," Mandie teased.

"You have rats in this house?" Jonathan asked quickly.

"Lots of them. Didn't you hear them running around under your bed last night?" Joe joked.

"Snowball would not allow a rat to live in this house," Sallie added.

Later as they sat through the noon meal, Mandie

wondered why Jonathan was so interested in seeing every little piece of the big house. This curiosity streak didn't seem natural for Jonathan Guyer. Maybe he was up to something. She would have to keep close watch on him and see.

Chapter 12 / Secret Revealed

After the noon meal was over, Polly came over to the Shaw house.

"I've had to stay home because of our company, Mother said," Polly told the young people in the sitting room. "But I have permission to visit with y'all this afternoon."

"That's good, Polly," Mandie said with a slight smile. "Because Jonathan wants to see our attic and our cellar, and you can go with us."

"What on earth for?" Polly asked Jonathan.

"I showed Mandie my house when she came to see us, so now I want her to show me her house," Jonathan said with a big grin.

"But your house is big, like a museum or something, and ours is just a house," Mandie said. "But if you really want to see it, let's go. The attic first."

"To the attic, then," Jonathan agreed.

When they arrived all the way up at the attic, Jonathan didn't seem very interested in the place.

And then when they went down into the cellar, he still didn't have much to say. Mandie wondered why he really wanted to see those places.

They went back to the sitting room and talked about nothing in particular until it was time for supper.

"Polly, are you going to eat with us? We're going out caroling afterwards with Grandmother," Mandie explained after Liza had come to tell them, "it's on de table."

"I have to go home for supper because my mother said I could only stay for the afternoon, but I'll ask her about joining y'all later for caroling," Polly promised as she left.

As soon as supper was over, Polly returned to say her mother would allow her to go caroling with them and on to the church for the midnight service. The relatives were too old to go out at that time of night, so Mrs. Cornwallis would be staying home with them.

Later, as Mandie had expected, her grandmother joined right in with the young people in their walks around the town as they sang carols. And after that everyone went to the midnight church service.

When they returned to the house, they were all tired and decided to retire for the night. But Mandie, once she and Sallie were in her room, was wide awake and wanted to talk. She told Sallie she was suspicious of Jonathan's wanderings about the house.

"I have an idea," Mandie said. "Let's go hide in the hallway and watch and see if he comes out and goes anywhere besides his room."

"Do you think we should?" Sallie asked.

"Why not? We won't be doing anyone any harm," Mandie insisted. "Come on. We'll have to be extra quiet." She started for the door, looking back to be sure Snowball was curled up asleep on her bed and wouldn't follow them.

"There's a little alcove right down here on the way to Jonathan's room," Mandie whispered as they crept quietly down the hallway. "We can wait in there and watch. If he leaves his room, he will have to come right by it." They came to the place just large enough for two chairs and a small table, and they sat down.

Mandie and Sallie had not been there long when, sure enough, Jonathan came silently down the corridor. And he was carrying what looked like Christmas presents wrapped in red paper.

"He's probably going to put those under the tree," Mandie whispered in Sallie's ear. But as they watched, he went up the stairs instead of down toward the parlor.

"Come on," Mandie said. She stood up and watched until Jonathan was out of sight, and then she softly followed with Sallie behind her.

When they got to the landing on the third floor, Mandie thought they had lost Jonathan because he was nowhere in sight. Then she heard a slight noise and realized he had entered Uncle John's office. How had he been able to do that? It was supposed to be kept locked.

While the girls stooped behind a large chair in the hallway, Jonathan came back out. He didn't even pause but immediately went to the staircase and on up to the attic. Mandie and Sallie followed silently. The halls were dark except for a lamp that was left burning for the night.

"What is he doing?" Mandie whispered as he disappeared up the steps.

When they got to the landing, Mandie could see Jonathan in the light of the moon that was coming in from the window. He opened the door to the attic, put something inside, and then started back down the stairway. Mandie and Sallie had to scramble for cover behind a tall statue as he passed them and went back down the stairs.

Mandie and Sallie followed him again. This time he went all the way down to the main floor and on to the back stairs that went down to the cellar. He walked quickly to the cellar door, opened it, and disappeared down the steps. The girls stayed hidden behind the hall tree at the back door and watched as he immediately came back out and closed the door. This time he was empty-handed. He hurried toward the staircase and went up the steps.

"He's hiding something!" Mandie whispered as they stayed a safe distance behind him and also went on up the staircase. They watched him go into his room and close the door.

"Come on," Mandie whispered to Sallie as she started up the staircase to the third floor.

The girls went into John Shaw's office through the door that should have been locked, and in the dim light Mandie saw one of the red-wrapped packages sitting on the desk. She went straight to it, picked it up, turned it over and over, but could not decide what was inside.

"These must be Christmas presents, but I don't see any name on this one," Mandie said in a soft voice. "I wonder what he is up to. This sure is a strange way to act."

"Perhaps the present is for your uncle," Sallie said.

"Maybe, but who would the presents in the attic and the cellar be for?" Mandie said thoughtfully. "He is playing tricks for some reason."

Suddenly the answer came. Mandie looked at Sallie in the dim light, and Sallie smiled. Together the girls said, "The treasure map! Jonathan sent the treasure map!"

"But how did he know where to hide the presents?" Sallie asked. "He has never visited here before."

"Let's go down to the parlor and look at the treasure map," Mandie said, quietly closing the door.

The girls rushed silently down to the parlor. Mandie took the lid off the box she had received, and together they studied the indentations in the dirt. Mandie almost screamed with excitement when she realized those little ruts were not roads outside but the hallways in her house.

"Hallways, not roads!" she told Sallie. "But we still don't know how he knew the layout of our house."

"That is a mystery," Sallie said as they stood there looking at the map.

Mandie yawned and said, "I suppose we'd better go to bed because everyone will be up early."

The two girls went to bed, but it was a long time before Mandie went to sleep. How had Jonathan known the layout of her house? And why did he do such a thing? Now that she thought about it, he had not seemed anxious to join the treasure hunt outdoors. No wonder! He knew it was inside the house.

As usual, on Christmas morning everyone in the

household was up early and assembled in the parlor to exchange gifts. John Shaw always gave his servants a pay increase on this day in addition to a present for each one.

Mandie watched the presents under the tree being passed around to the proper person, and she didn't see the three packages that Jonathan had put in those odd places the night before. Finally, when the last one was given out, Jonathan looked at Mandie and said with a big grin, "I brought presents for you, your mother, your uncle John, and your grandmother, but you will have to find them. That's what the treasure map is about." He was sitting beside Joe on the settee, and the girls were seated nearby.

Mandie shook her finger at him and grinned back as she said, "Sallie and I know where every one of those presents is, but I'd like to know how you were able to draw a treasure map of the inside of our house when you've never been here."

"That was easy," Jonathan said, still grinning. "You see, you introduced me to Dr. Plumbley in New York, and he used to live on your property here and was familiar with the layout of the house. So I talked to him about it. He thought it was a great idea, by the way."

"Wait till I see Dr. Plumbley again!" Mandie exclaimed.

"Well, are you going to get the presents or not?" Jonathan asked.

Mandie stood up and said, "Come on, Sallie, let's go."

The girls left the room and Jonathan followed. When they went into John Shaw's office, Mandie asked, "Why is Uncle John's office unlocked? He always keeps it locked."

"He left it unlocked because I told him I would like to borrow a book out of here," Jonathan said, pointing to the rows of books along the walls. "I did borrow a book to read after I went to bed."

Mandie picked up the red-wrapped present on the desk and asked, "Who is this supposed to be for?" The present was a little heavy.

"Your uncle John and your mother, of course, since this is his office," Jonathan said. "Now, go ahead and find the others."

The girls led the way up to the attic next. When Mandie pushed the door open, she spotted the red-wrapped present just inside on a small table. Picking it up she asked, "And whose is this?"

"That's for your grandmother," Jonathan replied.

The gift felt awfully light. Whatever was inside didn't weigh much.

"Now for the last one," Jonathan said.

The three went down the cellar steps, and Mandie found the third gift sitting on the bottom step. She picked it up and asked, "And this?"

"That's for you, and please don't drop it. It might break," Jonathan warned her.

"I suppose we should take all these things back to the parlor," Mandie said.

"Yes, and I want to see your grandmother's face when she unwraps hers," Jonathan said with a big grin.

When the three of them entered the parlor, the adults were talking, but Mandie interrupted. "Excuse me, Mother, everyone, but we have some presents here. They are from Jonathan." She went to her mother and handed her the one she had found in Uncle John's office. "For you and Uncle John."

She walked over to her grandmother and said, "This one is for you." And the last one she still held in her hand as she started to unwrap it.

Elizabeth had opened the gift and called across the room to Jonathan, "Thank you so much for this book about New York. I'm sure John and I will enjoy reading it."

"Yes, I know we will. Thank you," John Shaw added.

Mrs. Taft was taking off what seemed to be layers and layers of paper, and finally she came to the contents of the package. "My, my!" she exclaimed, shaking out an apron and holding it up. "I don't believe I've ever owned one of these."

"You have everything else, so I thought that would be something you didn't have," Jonathan explained with a big grin.

"And I intend to use it. Amanda has said she would teach me to cook. Can you imagine that? I have never learned to cook," Mrs. Taft said, laughing as she examined the delicate embroidery around the edge of the apron.

"That's because you've never had to," Lindall Guyer said with a loud laugh.

Mrs. Taft gave him a look, but Mandie couldn't interpret the meaning.

Suddenly the song, "I Love You Truly," blasted across the room. Mandie quickly spotted a Graphophone sitting on a table in the corner, and although he tried to move away from it, she was sure Jonathan had been the one who had turned on the machine.

John Shaw quickly went over and turned down the sound. "This is my present for Elizabeth," he said, looking at the startled faces across the room.

Mandie noticed Mrs. Taft was fingering the apron and was not looking at anyone. Evidently she didn't like the music.

Mandie thought about what she had done. She had deceived her grandmother because she didn't speak up and say she had invited the Guyers when Mrs. Taft had remarked that she wondered why Elizabeth had not told her they were coming. She needed to talk to Uncle Ned, but Jonathan was waiting for her to unwrap the last gift which was for her.

"Come on, Mandie," Jonathan urged her as she stood there holding the present. "Look inside."

Mandie glanced at him and quickly tore off the wrapping. Her blue eyes got big as she looked at the Brownie box camera in her hand. She had heard all about these cameras and had wanted one.

"Oh, thank you, Jonathan, thank you!" Mandie exclaimed, hugging the camera to her.

"Watch out. There's film in the package, too. You can take six pictures on one roll of film," Jonathan explained.

"I'll have to try it out while everyone is visiting here," Mandie said as she pulled out the film.

Jonathan stepped forward and inserted the film into the camera for her. "Now all you have to do is aim and press the button," he said. "But not in here. It's too dark. You should use it outdoors in the daylight."

"Oh, I will," Mandie promised. She glanced at Uncle Ned again, and this time he caught her look. She smiled and nodded toward the door. He understood and went into the hallway.

As soon as she could get away from Jonathan, Mandie followed Uncle Ned and found him in the sitting room. She sat down next to him.

"Oh, Uncle Ned, I've done a terrible thing," she began. "And I don't know how to straighten everything out."

"What Papoose do?" the old man asked.

"I was deceitful with my grandmother," Mandie began. "You see, she said to me that she wondered why Mother had not told her she had invited the Guyers to visit here, when all the time I was the one who invited them, and I didn't explain to her. I let her believe my mother did it so she wouldn't be angry with me. For some reason she doesn't like the Guyers."

"That happened long time ago," Uncle Ned said. "But she must tell you reason, not my business. Now you must go to her and explain and ask her forgiveness. And you must ask Great God to forgive, too."

"I know, but I'm a little afraid of what my grandmother will do," Mandie said, nervously clutching the old man's hand. "She has strong likes and dislikes. You know that."

"But still have to tell her, right away," Uncle Ned insisted. He stood up. "Go now."

"Couldn't I ask God to forgive me first?" Mandie said, rising from her seat and looking up at the tall man.

"Yes, we talk to Big God," Uncle Ned said, grasping her hand and looking upward. "Big God, Papoose has done wrong to grandmother. Ask forgiveness for her."

Mandie also looked upward and added, "Dear God, I'm sorry I misled my grandmother. Somehow I am always doing wrong things. Please keep my feet on the straight and narrow path. And please

forgive me this time. I thank you with all my heart."
She squeezed Uncle Ned's hand and said, "I'd better go and find Grandmother."

"Yes," the old man said. "And remember next
time. Think before act."

"I'm sorry, Uncle Ned, and I love you," Mandie
said, squeezing his hand with both of hers, and then
she turned to hurry back into the hallway and to the
parlor.

Mrs. Taft was rising from her chair and saying,
"I need to go to my room for a few minutes, but I
will be back in time for breakfast."

Mandie stopped at the doorway and waited until
Mrs. Taft had come out into the hall. She walked
along with her as she headed toward the stairway.

"I need to talk to you a minute, Grandmother,"
Mandie told her as they ascended the stairs.

Mrs. Taft looked down at her and said, "I'm sorry
I've been so busy, dear. I know you've been trying
to talk to me ever since we got here. Come on. Let's
go to my room."

Once they were inside Mrs. Taft's room, she mo-
tioned for Mandie to sit down beside her. "Now,
Amanda, what is it you want to talk about?" she
asked.

Mandie looked up at her and said, "I'm afraid I
have deceived you, Grandmother. I let you believe
my mother invited the Guyers when I was the one
who invited them. I was sorry as soon as I asked
them, though, because I know for some reason you
don't like Mr. Guyer, but I couldn't cancel my invitation."

"Why, Amanda, you invited the Guyers?" Mrs.
Taft repeated, looking at her. "You mean you invited
the Guyers without asking your mother first?"

"Yes, ma'am, I did," Mandie admitted. "I invited them while I was visiting at their house in New York during Thanksgiving, and then I wrote and told Mother what I had done. She said it was all right, that she would write and tell them they would be welcome."

"Well!" Mrs. Taft exclaimed, evidently at a loss of words. Then she added, "I hate to tell you this, but you will have to inform your mother."

"I know," Mandie agreed. "Will you please forgive me? I'm really and truly sorry."

Mrs. Taft looked at her silently for a moment and then said, "No harm done. But mind you, don't do such a thing again, you hear?"

Mandie smiled at her and said, "Thank you, Grandmother."

"Now I have some things to do here. You go back to your friends," Mrs. Taft said as she stood up.

"Yes, Grandmother," Mandie replied as she walked toward the door.

Stepping out into the hallway, Mandie saw her mother going into her room down the corridor. She turned around toward her grandmother and said, "I see my mother now. I'll go get her."

She hurried to catch her mother and asked her to come to Mrs. Taft's room with her. Elizabeth questioned her but went along.

When the situation was explained to Elizabeth, she was not as lenient as her mother had been. She was clearly upset. "Amanda, you must straighten up and try to live a better, more honest life. Because of your deception, I am forbidding you to ever invite anyone to this house without first coming to me. Do you understand that? If I cannot trust you to be honest, then I will have to restrain some of those impulses you have.''

"Yes, Mother,'' Mandie said meekly. "I understand and I am sorry.''

Elizabeth looked at her mother and then at Mandie. "Now go back down to the parlor. Your friends are waiting for you there,'' she said.

Mandie got up to leave the room and walked slowly to the door. Looking back, she said, "I am truly sorry, Mother and Grandmother.''

Mandie slowly made her way back to the parlor with the guilty feeling that she had let her grandmother and her mother down. She was disgusted with herself.

Then when she got to the parlor door, she heard Dr. Woodard saying to Mr. Guyer and Uncle John, "Yes, Joe will definitely go away to college somewhere next year. We are still looking and don't know where yet, but he will go somewhere.''

Mandie felt another stab at her heart. Her lifetime friend, Joe Woodard, was going away and would not be coming for frequent visits as he had always done. She would have no one to help solve all the mysteries she kept running into—except her friend Celia. But then Celia very seldom came to Mandie's house, not like Joe did.

Yes, she was going to miss Joe, more than anyone knew.